ABSOLUTE POWER

JEANA E. MANN

"Power is of two kinds: one is obtained by the fear of punishment and the other by acts of love." –Mahatma Gandhi

Preface

CASH

"Please." Her pouty mouth trembles on the plea as I bend her over the back of my sofa and gaze down at her plump ass. Legs spread apart. Naked. Fearful but willing.

"Please, what?" I trail a fingertip down the groove of her spine, loving the way her smooth skin erupts in gooseflesh. With her hands tied behind her, she's submissive and needy. Just the way I've fantasized a million times.

"Please fuck me." The tremble in her voice gives me all the power in this bizarre relationship of struggle and revenge.

This woman stole from me. Humiliated me. Threatened my reputation. I went after her in a quest for revenge, but I didn't realize her lips would taste like wine, or her body would beg to be dominated. Equal parts of anger and desire war inside my head. She owes me. I want her. Why is this so damn complicated? Why am I more concerned about her happiness than my reputation? It makes no sense.

Maybe I've lost my edge. At this moment, nothing matters more than her. I wrap my fingers around her neck, lift her to a standing position, and lower my lips to her ear. "You only had to ask for it."

I awake from the dream, sweating, with a painful erection tenting the sheet. Not only does this dark-eyed angel haunt my reality, she's managed to infiltrate my sleep. I can't eat. I can't think. I can't even get a good night's rest because of her. With a groan of frustration, I climb out of bed and walk to the window overlooking the lake. This madness has to end, and it can only come to one conclusion. By the end of the summer, I'll own her body, mind, and soul.

ONE

Jagger
_____

T he bell over the door to Mercer's Fine Jewelry and Art Gallery jingles. A stranger crosses the threshold. I curse under my breath at the interruption to my nightly routine. I should've locked the door at closing. Before tonight, it's never been necessary. Few people venture out after dark in Baxter's Corner, Indiana. In fact, you might say this small, sleepy community rolls up the sidewalks and shuts down when the sun hits the horizon. That's why I chose this place as my home. Low key. No hassle. Quiet.

"We're closed." I toss the remark over my shoulder, not bothering to look up from the dust mop in my hands.

"The sign says you're open." The grit in the deep, masculine voice entices me to turn around. This isn't our usual type of customer. He's tall, the crown of his head almost grazing the top of the door frame. A black denim jacket showcases his broad shoulders. He lowers the hood of his sweatshirt to reveal dark, close-cropped hair. A pulse of attraction hits me straight between the thighs. *Strange.* I haven't had a tingle down there in months.

Sensing my desire, he flashes a shy grin. Lo and behold, two fathomless dimples appear in his cheeks. Beneath his tough guy exterior, his smile holds boyish appeal.

"Um, no worries. I forgot to flip the sign." I smile back and rest the handle of the dust mop against the nearest display case. "What can I do for you?"

He bends at the knees to get a better look at my name badge. "Jagger? Unusual name." The line of his lips tightens for a fraction of a second.

"Yeah, my mom was into the Rolling Stones." Before she became a substance abuser. Before she abandoned me and my older sister Calliope.

He takes a step closer and extends a hand for me to shake. The movement draws my attention to the tattoos there. A skull and snake wrapped around a knife. Above the collar of his shirt, a hawk centers above the notch in his collarbone, wings wrapping around the column of his neck. Gang style tattoos like those worn by members of DOR, the Disciples of Rage. I've heard of Chicago gangs moving south into Indiana, looking for recruits in the smaller towns, and forcing shop owners to pay money for protection. I never thought it would happen here.

My stomach clenches. I hesitate, but he goes the extra few inches and slides his palm against mine. His touch is warm and confident, sending an unexpected prickle through my fingers. After a second, he releases me then shoves both hands deep into the pockets of his blue jeans. The smile drops from his face. An impending sense of danger flashes through me.

"I don't want any problems." The breathiness in my voice betrays my anxiety. I'm not sure what bothers me more, the glittering dark of his eyes or his air of implacable confidence.

"Neither do I." The scratchiness in his baritone creates an itch in my core, one that can only be resolved by sex. Hot, *hot* sex with me bent over the textile table and my panties around my ankles.

I lick the dryness from my lips and glance at the phone resting on the counter. Too far away to be helpful. One deep breath helps steady my nerves. "The town cop will be by for a security check any minute." A total lie.

He shrugs. "I haven't broken any laws, have I? I'm just a dude who loves fine jewelry and art." As he speaks, he studies the framed black-and-white picture on the wall. He clasps his hands behind his back. "This is nice. Who's the photographer?"

"Stella Valentine." The words crackle from my tight throat. "That's the covered bridge from the next town down the road." Maybe I'm overreacting. If life has taught me anything, it's to expect the unexpected. Plenty of people have judged me for my appearance. I don't want to be one of them. He deserves the benefit of the doubt. Together, we admire the sharp focus and tonal range of the photograph. "She's local. Very talented. She does a lot of work for *National Geographic*. Some people think she's going to be the next Ansel Adams." I trace the picture frame with a fingertip. Scoring an original Stella Valentine for the gallery was a highlight of my job. "If you like this, she has more. We're thinking of having a show this summer."

"I like it. What else you got?" He steps around me to study the hand thrown pottery on the shelf behind us. The tension eases from my shoulders. His interest seems sincere. I feel like a judgmental ass.

"Everything in here is from local artists and craftsmen." For a few seconds, my enthusiasm for the work overrides my distrust. "There are metal sculptures in the next room and jewelry in the room beyond that."

"Yeah?" Through double thick lashes, he casts a panty-melting side glance in my direction. "What kind of jewelry?"

"Rings, necklaces, pendants, precious gems, and diamonds." I smile, unable to curb my flirtatious tone. Sexy guys are few and far between in Baxter's Corner. "Is there anything specific you're interested in?"

"Maybe. I'll know it when I see it."

"Okay. I'm here if you have any questions."

"Thanks, Jagger." The way he says my name sends a pleasant wave of goosebumps along my arms. His dark eyes sweep over me, assessing and enigmatic. "I'll do that."

Once his back is to me, I sweep my phone from the counter and into my pocket. I retrieve the dust mop and run it over the worn pine floor, trailing along behind him. Although my gaze is lowered toward my work, I watch him through my lashes. He scrutinizes each display, tilting his head to capture the creations from different angles, until he comes to the jewelry cases.

"These are good." He taps a fingernail on the glass above an arrangement of necklaces and rings. "Who makes these?"

"Me," I croak, clear my throat, and try again. "I do."

"Really?" His eyebrows lift. "Think you could do some custom work for me? I wanna make something for my grandma's birthday."

"Sure." Although he's not exactly the kind of customer I was hoping to attract, I can use the work. And how cute is he—talking about his grandma? "We can sit down and create something together, or you can send me a picture of what she likes. I can make just about anything."

The dimples return, bracketing his wide mouth. "Pretty *and* talented. You're quite a girl, Jagger."

"Thanks." My cheeks warm under his praise, which is almost as confusing as his interest in the custom jewelry.

"I'm curious." A few strides brings him inside my personal space. The scent of spicy cologne teases my nose. Up close, his toned, athletic body is intimidating. I press my thighs together, fighting away the moisture gathering in my panties. He cocks his head. "How does a girl like you get into a business like this?"

"Um, well, I've always liked art. Especially fine jewelry. And my sister was in the business." As a jewel thief, but that's another story. A tug at my subconscious warns me to stop talking. Oversharing to a gang-type thug isn't the smartest idea.

"But you do all the work, right?" He shoves his hands into his pockets again and stares down at me. "I mean, you run the place."

"Yes, I'm the manager. Mr. Mercer is getting up there in years and wants to retire. He taught me everything I know about the business and jewelry design."

"Come to think of it, I think you made a piece for my friend. A platinum ring with a four-carat simulated ruby surrounded by cubic zirconias. High quality. Very unique. In fact, most jewelers wouldn't know it's a fake." The intensity of his stare does crazy things to my insides. "I've got a picture of it on my phone. Let me show you." A knot begins to form in the pit of my stomach. I glance down at the floor. He hands the phone to me, but one glance is all I need to recognize the entwined vines engraved on the band, the crisscross gallery, the flawless simulated stones.

"Um, it's very pretty, but no. It wasn't me." The lie doesn't discourage him.

"Are you sure?" He flashes those panty-dropping dimples. "He said he got it here a few weeks ago." Even though his hands remain in his pockets, the threat of danger emanates from the coiled strength in his muscles. "Sorry if I'm being pushy. I was just really impressed by the craftsmanship, and my grandma deserves the best."

"No. It's okay." My stomach churns. "I'd remember something like that." How could I forget? That particular piece took a month to make.

"Ah, well." His gaze dips to my lips, and holy hell, I'm dumbstruck by the promise of his full mouth on mine. Now is not the time for sexual fantasies, however. I need to get him out of here. Pronto. He shakes his head. "That's disappointing. Because I'm very, *very* interested in meeting the person who made it."

"Are you a cop?" The question arrives in a whisper, barely audible. Dozens of scenarios play out in my head. None of them end in my favor.

His laughter rings through the empty room. "Do I look like a cop to you, Jagger?"

"No." *Damn.* I roll my lips together. The ring had been the latest in a string of forgeries. I'd seen it in the window of a premier jewelry store in upscale Carmel. When I went home, I made a copy. A month later, I walked back into the place, asked to see the ring, and—when the salesgirl turned her back—swapped the forgery for the real one. The thrill had been unbelievable. I never thought anyone would find out. Especially not a sexy-as-sin tatted-up gangbanger.

"What were you looking for?" Emeline, our sales-person/accountant, strides into the room from the rear of the store on a cloud of cold air. She'd left work an hour ago to get ready for her date and wasn't supposed to be back until her shift tomorrow morning. Her hazel eyes take note of the man standing in my personal space and flicker to my face, questioning. "Is everything okay?" With a sigh of relief, she grabs her phone from the shelf beneath the counter. "There it is. I knew I left it here."

The stranger's expression brightens. "I'm looking

for the person who made this ring. Your girl here doesn't recall, but maybe you do." He holds up his phone. Em leans forward to study the picture.

"Oh, yeah. Sure, I remember. Jagger made it." She's too enamored with his dimples to notice my dismay.

"Is that right?" His even white teeth bite into the fullness of his lower lip. Plush, soft, kissable lips. "Jagger seems to have forgotten."

"Seriously, Jag? You worked on it for weeks and—" The rest of her words die on her lips when she catches the panic in my eyes. She makes a strangled chirp and clears her throat. "Or maybe not. Who knows. I'm an airhead."

"Must've been a mix-up," the guy replies with an easy shrug of those wide shoulders. "Too bad."

"Did you need anything else, Em?" I ask her, eager to get her out of the store before she gets me into more trouble.

"Um, no. That's it." She backs toward the employee entrance. "But I can stay if you need me." Her worried glance bounces between me and the smoldering bad boy. "Tony's waiting in the car. I can ask him to come back in a bit."

"No. I'm fine. You can go." I summon a deep breath to calm my nerves. No damage has been done—yet. With a little luck, this guy will leave and no one will ever know what I've done.

"Are you sure?" She sucks her bottom lip between her teeth.

"Absolutely. This gentleman was on his way out."

"Okay, well, see you later." Her high heels click on the wood floor as she leaves.

"Nice to meet you. Enjoy your evening," the man calls after her. If he wasn't so intimidating, he'd be absolutely charming.

Once she's safely out of earshot, evicting this sexy thug becomes my top priority. I smile and try to crowd him in the direction of the exit. "I apologize for the mix-up. She gets confused easily. Mr.—I'm sorry? I didn't catch your name." He doesn't reply, just gives me a strange knowing look like he has a secret—one I'm not going to enjoy. I nod toward the door. "If you don't mind, it's getting late, and I really do need to close up."

"All right." He walks to the front door. I trail on his heels, intending to secure the store the minute he crosses the threshold. Instead of leaving, he locks the door and draws the shade. When he turns around, the corners of his eyes crinkle, but there's no sign of humor on his face. I'm less than two yards from him with nowhere to run. His dark eyes lock with mine. "Let's get real for a minute, Jagger."

He walks up to me, his strides slow and easy. The tips of his black-and-white Chuck Taylor's stop millimeters from my scuffed ballet flats. Up close, I can see the stubble on his cheeks, the small scar above his left eyebrow, and the black lines of the tattoo curling around his neck. Fear chills my blood. I've seen that look before in my ex-boyfriend's eyes. It's the look of a man with an agenda—one that won't play out in my favor. He drags the backs of his fingers down my cheek in a soft caress then wraps them around my throat. The blockage of blood through my arteries creates spots before my eyes.

"Please don't hurt me," I croak. "We don't have any money. We've already made the bank deposit for the day."

"Why would I want to hurt a pretty little thing like you?" He releases my throat. Adrenaline races through my veins. Under different circumstances, I'd swoon over the way he tucks a loose strand of my hair behind my ear. His touch, although gentle, disguises a threat. "I'm just here to talk."

"About what?" In my wildest dreams, I can't come up with a valid reason for his presence. If he's not a cop, then why is he asking these questions?

"You stole from me, Jagger." He straightens the collar of my blouse. "Now what are we gonna do about this?"

"I don't have any idea what you're talking about." The shaking in my body intensifies until I'm sure he can hear my teeth chattering.

He inches closer, forcing me to tilt my head up to look at him. My body tingles, acutely aware of his size, his strength, his maleness. Although my common sense is screaming to escape, my body angles toward him in a primal urge to mate. The width of his shoulders blocks out the rest of the room. His cologne, expensive and masculine, carries hints of citrus and rain. *Delicious.*

"About a month ago, someone came into my store, switched out this ruby ring for a fake, and walked away.

A pretty girl with long, dark hair and big, baby doll eyes." His gaze caresses my face, my breasts, before returning to my mouth. That look is *everything*—sin and seduction and promise rolled up inside a pretty bad boy exterior. "So, I started asking around. It wasn't very hard to find you." Between his thumb and index finger, he rolls one of my errant curls. "You've got some big balls, baby girl."

"It wasn't me." My skin burns where his fingertips brushed my shoulder. I take a step backward. "I'm sure there's a reasonable—"

"Don't deny it. I've got you on video." His eyes grow darker, predatory like a wolf. Guilt tightens my chest. I'd been so careful to keep my face away from the camera. He must have more than one in the showroom.

As the gap closes between us, I struggle to breathe. His gaze narrows. "Did you think I wouldn't come looking for you?" When I don't answer, he creeps forward. I retreat until my back hits the wall. He places his palms flat against the plaster on each side of my head, trapping me between two strong arms. "I want the original ring or the money."

The tightness in my throat makes it difficult to speak. "The ring is gone. I sold it. But I've got four thousand in my bank account. I can write you a check. Just—please don't tell anyone."

"A check?" He shakes his head. "I only deal in cash and diamonds, sweetheart. Besides, the way I see it, you owe me a little over two hundred grand."

Bile burns the back of my throat. Yes, I took the

ring, and yes, he's due compensation, but he's crazy if
he thinks I owe him two hundred thousand dollars.
"That ring wasn't worth more than five."

"True, but there's also the matter of the money your
sister stole from me." Cunning sparkles in his eyes.
"And since you're here and she's not, I'll collect from
you."

The world I've built for myself comes crashing to
my feet. "You're Cash Delacorte." Calliope's ex-
boyfriend. The one who took her out of the strip club
and turned her into a high society cat burglar. The man
she ran from and never looked back. Tension stabs
between my shoulder blades.

"Damn straight, I am." His stare burns through me,
through my defenses, through my courage. "Did you
think I wouldn't come looking for you?" The heat from
his large body seeps through my clothing and into my
soul, igniting a fire of danger and desire. "So how we
gonna settle this? The way I see it, you owe five thousand for the ring. Two hundred grand for your sister's
debt."

My stomach drops. Maybe, if I sold my Honda, I
could come up with five grand, but *two hundred thousand dollars*? There's no way. "I—I don't have that kind
of money."

He smirks. The gesture might have been adorable
under different circumstances. "Tell you what. I'm
feeling generous today. Forget the ring. Let's make it an
even two hundred G's, and we'll call it a day."

Callie never said much about Cash. She kept that

part of her life secret from me. Now I know why. He's terrifying and charming and cunning. After a deep breath, I summon my courage and stare back into his deep brown eyes. "I'll pay you for the ring, but I don't know anything about Calliope's debt, and I won't be responsible for it."

"Oh, girl." One of his eyebrows lifts like he's shocked at my refusal. His chuckle reverberates through my body and straight to the space between my legs. "You don't get to decide that."

"And what if I don't pay you?"

With an easy push, he retreats from me and the wall and returns his hands to his pockets. "In my line of work, it ain't no big thing to make a person disappear."

My brain races through options and scenarios. None of them end well. "I—I don't have that kind of cash, but if you give me a little time, I can come up with the money for the ring."

"Two hundred grand, Jagger. That's the deal. Either you pay up, or you don't. Your choice. You've got one week." He sighs, letting his shoulders drop. "Well, guess I've tied up enough of your time." Noiselessly, he pivots and strides toward the door. But his departure doesn't bring relief. If he's sincere—and I believe he is—this situation is far from over. Halfway to the exit, he pauses, glancing over his shoulder at the covered bridge photo-graph. "How much?"

"What?"

"For the Stella Valentine. How much?"

"Um, three thousand?"

"I'll take it as payment for the ring." I watch in mute shock as he removes the picture from its hanger, tucks it beneath his arm, and unlocks the door. At the threshold he pauses again. His voice is so quiet that I have to lean forward to hear his words. "I'll be in touch."

TWO

Cash

G age gives me a sideways glance from behind the wheel of the Escalade. I slouch down in the seat, ignoring his questioning gaze. He knows me well enough to stay quiet. I reach across the console and turn up the volume of the stereo until the windows rattle. Tiny snowflakes whirl in the headlights as we speed out of the small town.

We're halfway home before he shuts off the music. "So, how did it go?" Like always, he's got a knit cap pulled down low over his forehead. Back when we were kids, he'd been a scrawny, pretty boy, and I'd been the bully. Not anymore. He towers over me by a few inches, and his biceps are the size of small melons. That's why he's the muscle, and I'm the brains. Just the sight of him would make a man piss his pants.

"Not like I expected." I shift in the plush bucket seat, trying to find a comfortable position, one that eases the rage and confusion banging against my ribs.

"What does that mean?" He flicks another glance at me. "Is she like Calliope?"

"They look alike." Same long dark hair, olive complexion, and round ass. The similarities end there. While Callie has a sharpness about her, Jagger is the picture of sweetness. "She's got the same smart ass mouth."

Gage chuckles. "That explains a lot." He met Callie a few days before me. The three of us were tight for close to a decade. Our friendship made her betrayal a bitter pill to swallow. "Did you get the money or not?"

"It's gonna be more complicated than we thought." The original plan had been to teach this girl a lesson. A man in my business can't allow a debt to go unpaid. I'd been prepared to make an example of her until I caught a whiff of her powdery sweet perfume and touched her velvet skin. My dick gets hard at the memory. I adjust the fly of my jeans and try to forget the image of her pouty mouth.

"I still think you should go after Callie for the money. She's the thief, not her little sis."

"Callie's Russian mafia boyfriend has her locked up tight in his Manhattan penthouse. I'll never get close to her. But her sister? She's a different story. Besides, going after Jagger sends the message that friends and family are fair game if you fuck with me."

Gage tugs off his knit cap, tosses it aside, releasing his blond wavy hair. He scrubs a hand over his scalp. "You want me to have a chat with Jagger?"

"No. I'll take care of it." In fact, I can't wait to see her again.

THREE

Jagger

T he instant Cash steps over the threshold, I jog to the door and flip the lock. Through the display window, I watch him climb into a black Escalade. He pulls away from the curb. The taillights disappear down the street. I set the security alarm and rush out the back. Once I arrive home, I lock all the doors and windows, close the curtains, and sit in the darkness of my bedroom with my knees pulled to my chest and my arms wrapped around them.

My first instinct is to call Calliope, except I don't have her phone number. When we parted, she made me promise not to contact her. That's how terrified she was of Cash. I know the general vicinity of her location. She has a rich new boyfriend in Manhattan. If she wanted to find me, she could. She has the resources and the money. Part of me is hurt that she hasn't reached out, but the other part understands. Her desperate attempt to escape Cash had worked, and she had the selflessness to provide me with this new life. Only she failed to explain the lockbox full of money belonged to him.

Now he's after me. Not only do I have to come up with two hundred thousand dollars, I've got to figure out a way to pay for the Stella Valentine photo tucked beneath his arm. The thought of lying to Mr. Mercer, a kind and generous man, is almost worse than Cash's retribution. Mr. Mercer can never know.

Emeline comes home a little after midnight. I'm still wide awake. She's been dating Tony for a few weeks. Their relationship seems to be going pretty well. I haven't met him yet, but her smiles say everything. I hear her footsteps along the hallway on the way to her room. I hold my breath until her door closes. In the morning, I wait until she goes for a run to take my shower then escape to the store before she returns.

I'm staring out the display window with unseeing eyes when Emeline arrives twenty minutes late. She breezes through the front door, bringing a gust of fresh chilly air along with her. "I know. I'm late." With a melodramatic sigh, she drops her purse on the counter and strips out of her coat and gloves to reveal a high-waisted pair of red slacks and a sleeveless, white, ruffled blouse. Smart and classy. "You won't believe what just happened. Mr. Johnson's cows got out of the pasture and trampled Margaret Madison's garden fence. She's so pissed. She got out her shotgun and started shooting at them. Don't worry. She's a terrible shot. Then Mr. Johnson tried to run over her with his pickup truck, and the police came, and I had to—" Her gaze lands on my face then the blank spot where the framed photo had been. "What's wrong? You're pale as a ghost. Where's the Stella Valentine photograph?"

"I sold it." My tone is flat and dejected, but she doesn't notice.

"Shut up. No way." After tossing her long, brown curls over her shoulder, she marches to the wall. It's a big deal. We haven't had more than a few sales in the last month. "The gangbanger guy?"

A war erupts between my conscience and the need for self-preservation. She would never tell a soul, but if I confess, she'll become a party to the deception, and I can't do that to her. I decide to remain cautious for the time being. "Yeah."

"Nice." The floorboards creak as she whirls and strides back to me. "He was hot. Scary but in a sexy way. I think he liked you."

Some of the tension eases out of my shoulders. If she's teasing me, she doesn't suspect anything. I roll my eyes. "You're crazy."

Mischief flickers in her clear eyes. "Did you guys have freaky kinky sex after I left?" She pats a hand on the counter. "Here?"

"Of course not." A flush heats my face because the thought had crossed my mind in that instant between his arrival and his ultimatum. To avoid her scrutiny, I flee to the backroom and begin unboxing a crate of handcrafted porcelain dolls.

Emeline follows me. "Did you tell Mr. Mercer about the sale?"

"No. His surgery was yesterday, remember?" The straw packing material crackles as I toss it aside.

"Oh, that's right. I hope everything went well." She gathers up the straw and stuffs it into a bag. "What about Stella? Does she know?"

"Not yet. She's in Tanzania on a photoshoot. I'll send her an email."

"Must be nice to travel the world with your hot husband." A heavy sigh gusts from between her pursed lips. "We should all be so lucky."

"Yeah." For a brief moment, I contemplate the luxury of overseas travel. I've always wanted to see the world. At this rate, I'll be lucky to see another morning. "I went to England once. With my sister. She was working there and took me along. We didn't really have time to sightsee, though." It had been a job for Cash, robbing the patrons of an elite masquerade ball, and the last time I saw Callie. At Heathrow Airport, she'd sent me on my way with a hug and the key to her lockbox.

"Really? That's cool." Em's brow furrows. "Wait a sec. You have a sister?"

"Yes." A lump tightens my throat. "But we haven't seen each other in years."

"Oh, honey, I'm sorry." Emeline crouches on her heels beside me and strokes a hand down my arm, empathy clouding her expression. "Why didn't you tell me?"

"It's okay." Four years hasn't lessened the emptiness in my chest left by Callie's absence. "We aren't in contact anymore."

"What happened?"

"It's complicated." Where would I even begin to recount the epic disaster of our lives? The parents who loved their addictions more than us. The grandmother who was kind to me but hated Callie. "She got mixed up with some bad people and started over with a new identity." Not exactly a lie, but not the truth either. To my knowledge, Cash had never laid a hand on her, and to his credit, he saved her from a life of prostitution. Other than that, Callie had kept the details of their relationship a secret.

"Why don't you give her a call?" The sorrow in her tone brings the sting of tears to my eyes. She stands, giving me an encouraging smile. "I'm sure she'd be thrilled to hear from you."

"No. I can't. We—I just can't. I don't even know her number." Although Emeline has been a trusted friend and employee for the past two years, no one knows the truth about my sister, and I plan to keep it that way. "I wouldn't want to endanger her new life."

"Well, it's her loss." Em takes one of the dolls and traces the round features with a fingertip. "These are cute. They should sell well. Do you have the details? I'll get them up on the website."

"Sure." With an inward sigh of relief, I hand her the packing slip. She hums to herself as she returns to the office. I continue to work, my hands operating through muscle memory while my mind searches for resolutions to my newest dilemma.

"Hey, I don't see the receipt for the photograph."

From my position in the backroom, her frown is evident. "Did he charge it or pay cash? The payment needs to hit the bank today. We're a little tight on making payroll. Also, I'd like to cut Stella's commission check since tomorrow is the end of the month, and I'll need to close out the books for February." A frown mars her forehead. "Even with that sale, we're not going to make a profit."

Damn, damn, *damn*. Heat rushes up my neck. "Um, that guy stayed forever. It was late and I didn't write it up like I should have, but I have the cash. I'll make the deposit at lunch."

"I can do it." She starts to roll her chair away from the desk.

"No." I spring to my feet then force myself to take a deep breath and relax. With a sheepish smile, I reply, "It's my fault. I'll do it. Why don't you finish putting the new inventory on the website, and I'll take care of the other. I have to take the deposit to the bank anyway."

At lunch, I make the hour drive into the city and get a high-interest short-term loan to pay for the Stella Valentine. Then I deposit the money into the store bank account. The weight of one lie is already an enormous burden, dragging my soul into the depths of unhappiness. I have to find a way out of this mess with Cash before anyone finds out.

On the way back to the store, I stop at the hospital to see Mr. Mercer. He's pale but chipper. His lined face brightens when I walk into his room. "There's my girl." His warm greeting doubles my guilt.

"Hi. I hear your surgery went well." I place the vase of fresh flowers on the dresser and squeeze his hand. "How are you feeling?"

"Better than I have a right to." His eyes crinkle at the corners. "Have a seat." He nods toward the chair at his bedside. "Is everything okay at the store? Have you sold anything?" I sandwich his hand between my palms and squeeze. Arthritis has warped his long, artistic fingers.

Guilt presses on my chest. "We sold the Stella Valentine last night." Anger at Cash bubbles in my veins. If Mr. Mercer knew, he'd be devastated, and I could never disappoint him. Borrowing the money to pay for the photo was the right thing to do.

"Excellent. I knew someone would jump on that thing. Did they squabble on the price? Do you think we should've marked it higher?" A worried frown deepens the creases on his forehead.

"No. Not at all." The warmth of his hand in mine fills my heart with regret. If he knew how stupid I've been, he'd never get over it.

"Ah, I'm thrilled." With a sigh of happiness, he reclines into the pillows. "And what about the Barrett Gems and Jewelry Trade Show in Las Vegas? Have you chosen your pieces yet?"

At his urging, I've entered a national trade show for gemologists. The best of the best will be there along with big name buyers. This could be the break we've been waiting for. Waves of nervous anticipation make my stomach twist. "I think so, but I'd like your input."

Using my phone, I show him photos of my proposed merchandise.

"Great choices." He nods in approval. "I only wish I could go with you."

"I'll be fine." I give him a reassuring smile. "You need to concentrate on getting better. We need you back at the store."

"You're doing so well, Jagger. I don't have any worries at all. Bringing you into the business was the best decision I ever made."

"Meeting you changed my life." I press the back of his hand to my cheek. Memories of my father are limited to his bouts of drunkenness and rage, but in my fantasies, I imagine a real father to be like Mr. Mercer— kind, patient, and warm. Remorse continues to build until my ribs ache. I don't deserve his praise.

"Mine too." His smile grows larger. "You're like a breath of fresh air after a thunderstorm." Tears shimmer in his eyes. "That's why I met with my lawyers last week to give you power of attorney over my affairs. I'm just not able to keep up anymore."

"No. You can't. I—"

"Stop. I won't listen to any arguments. It's what I want."

It's my turn for tears. "I'm flattered and grateful. But surely you have someone else? Another relative? A niece or nephew?" I don't deserve his kindness, not after what I've done. "You've worked too hard to give it all away to a stranger."

"Nonsense. You're more like family than any blood

kin. Besides, I lost touch with my family years ago."
Although we've had many long conversations since
meeting, he's never mentioned children or relatives. No
one has ever come to visit him at the store, and we've
always spent the holidays together.

"I understand."

"After Hattie passed on, I was just going through the
motions of living. We were married fifty-two years, you
know."

"I know," I reply softly. He's spoken of his wife
many times. Her photographs still cover the walls of his
apartment above the store. "She was lucky to have you."

"I was lucky to have *her*." A rusty chuckle grates
from his throat. "That woman gave me hell from sunup
to sundown, and I loved every minute of it. We met at
the state fair when I was a senior in high school and she
was a junior. She had a boyfriend at the time, but I
didn't care. From the moment I first laid eyes on her, I
knew she was going to be mine." Remembrance softens
his features. "Love like that only comes once in a
lifetime."

"Not for me. I can't even find a decent date." I huff
before slumping in my chair.

"You will."

"I always pick the worst guys." The external scars
left by Kyle's fists have healed, but the wounds to my
heart are still raw. Since then, I've kept my distance
from men.

"That's because you aren't listening to your heart.
You don't value yourself enough. Remember that." His

tone becomes stern. "And don't be swayed by pretty words. It's their actions that matter. A good man will care more about your well-being than his own."

The nurse enters the room, ending his lecture. We fall silent while she takes his blood pressure and checks his pulse. When she's finished, she gives me a polite smile. "Visiting hours are almost over, and Mr. Mercer needs his rest."

"Of course." I give his hand a final squeeze before standing. "I'll stop by and see you tomorrow."

"I'm looking forward to it." Exhaustion weights his eyelids. With a sigh, he settles into the pillows. He looks small, fragile, and pale against the white bed linens. I hate leaving him here alone. A flash of anger directed at his family stirs my temper. He deserves better. I consider contacting them before I reconsider. For now, I'll respect his wishes and leave them where they belong —in his past. Goodness knows, I understand.

FOUR

Jagger

The best parts of my day are the small, quiet moments in my house. The two-bedroom, one-bath cottage is the first place I've been able to claim as mine. *All* mine. No mortgage. No landlord. Just twelve hundred square feet of heaven to roam alongside Emeline and Lucy, my dog. With a sigh of satisfaction, I carry my coffee cup to the back deck and lean against the railing. Lucy sniffs around my feet. Like all Chihuahuas, she hates the cold and shivers incessantly, but her worries over the chilly air are tempered by her joy as a sparrow flits along the shrubbery. At the bottom of the sloping yard, the river winds its way toward the covered bridge. The gurgle of water playing over stones provides a soothing backdrop. I sigh before drawing in a deep breath of fresh country air.

Spring is days away, the snow has melted, and rebellious sprouts of hyacinths and daffodils push through the grass. In a few months, this cozy hamlet will be filled with tourists eager to visit the nearby art colony, galleries, and craft shops. With them, they'll bring a much-needed influx of cash to our struggling business.

The beauty of the evening is tempered by my anxiety over Cash. It's been six days since he came to the store. I don't have the money. When he calls, I'll explain the situation. He'll understand. He has to.

"Hey, get back here." Lucy tries to leap from the deck but skids to a stop. My command brings her back to my side. When I bend to pick her up, she licks my fingertips in a half-hearted apology. "Don't even think about it, missy."

My phone rings from the depths of my sweater pocket. It's Emeline again. She's called four times in the last hour to ask random questions. I scowl and accept the call. "What?"

"I need you to come down here. Right now."

"Why?" It's her turn to close the store. I've been looking forward to a quiet night of Netflix, solitude, and rest. "Can't it wait until the morning?"

"No." She draws out the single syllable to emphasize her impatience. "*He's* here."

"Who?" I straighten, set the coffee mug on the railing, and give her my full attention. It can't be him. I have another twenty-four hours to meet his deadline.

"You know who." She lowers her voice to a whisper. "He's asking for you."

My stomach does a tiny flip. "Okay. On my way."

When I get to the store, he's in the office with Emeline, his feet on the desk like he owns the place.

This time, he's wearing a black button-down shirt, tailored slacks, and a knit cap pulled low over his forehead. His eyes crinkle at the corners when I open the door. If I didn't know better, I'd swear he's happy to see me, and I have to admit, knowing he's attracted to me does crazy things to my insides.

"There you are. I hope I didn't interrupt anything important." His voice is quieter than I remember, a little hoarse and unsettling.

"No. It's fine. I just live down the street." I pat the messy bun on top of my head, wishing I'd taken the time to brush it out and put on makeup. The craziness of wanting to impress my extortionist is just another symptom of my fucked-up childhood. "What can I do for you?" His dark eyes cut sideways to Emeline then back to me. He wants her to leave. "Um, Em, could you go out front and clean the display cases?"

"You did that yesterday. I watched—" Catching my frown, she nods in understanding. "Sure. If you need anything, just holler."

Once she's out of earshot, Cash lifts an eyebrow. I swallow and prepare to make my case. "I don't have your money. Not yet."

"No?" From the back of his waistband, he withdraws a pistol and sets it on the desk with a clunk. I wince at the sound. I lick my lips and force myself to remain calm. Guys like this feed on fear. He sighs. "Try again."

"I've been thinking that maybe we could set up

some kind of payment arrangement. You know, an installment plan."

"Do I look like a lending institution to you, Jagger?" The solemn softness of his voice is more terrifying than the loudest scream. "You must have me confused with the Baxter's Corner Bank and Trust."

"No, of course not, but any reasonable person would understand—" I choke on the last word as he stands. In two swift strides he's around the desk and nose to nose with me, glaring down from his towering height.

"Don't talk to me about reasonable. Under the circumstances, I think I've been extremely understanding. Downright generous, in fact." His lips press into a thin line. He draws in a deep breath then exhales, like his patience is wearing thin.

"I don't have any money."

"Find a way to get it."

"I'm not rich." It's a struggle to keep the anger from my voice. "I make forty thousand a year. That's barely enough to live on. This store is struggling to stay above water. Even if I gave you every penny of my salary, it would take me five years to pay you off."

"Longer." A wry smirk twists the corners of his lips. "Don't forget the interest."

"I thought you weren't a bank." His chuckle reverberates through the room. I scowl. "It's not funny."

"Agreed. This is some serious shit." The way he licks his lips makes my knees weak. I place a hand on the counter to keep from melting onto the floor in a puddle of lust and fright. If only he were ugly or old or less *Cash*. His smirk doesn't help. "Maybe you should call your sister. She's the one who got you into this. I'd love a reunion."

"Not an option." The last thing I want is to involve Calliope. I can handle this. "We aren't in contact. We haven't spoken in years."

"That right?" He rubs his jaw with a tattooed hand. "I thought you two were tight."

"Not anymore." I duck my head in case the pain in my heart is visible on my face.

In a flash, his hand snakes to my throat. The metal edge of the desk bites into my bottom as he forces me backward. "Don't play games with me, Jagger." Spots swim in front of my eyes as his grip tightens, his thumb pressing on my jugular vein. I grip the edge of the desk with both hands to keep from tumbling backward. "Maybe we should call your pretty friend back in here. Is that what it will take to motivate you? Do I need to hurt someone you love?"

"Please," I croak. I'll do anything to keep Emeline safe.

His gaze flickers to my lips. Only for an instant but long enough for me to see the desire hidden there. He wants me. I'm sure of it. With a deep exhale, he releases my neck, backs away. "Now what are we going to do about this, Jagger? Tell me quick."

The seconds tick by slowly. The rush of blood in my ears drowns out the rapid beating of my heart. His thick eyelashes lower, shielding his thoughts. I have no doubt that he'll hurt me if I don't comply. "I don't have the money, but maybe I could pay you back another way."

He cocks his head, interest piqued. "Are we negotiating? You should know I don't do that."

"Um, well, I could make jewelry for you." It's a shitty suggestion, but I'm out of ideas, and it's the only talent I possess.

"You got the money to make jewelry but not the money to pay me?"

"Well, no, but I have a line of credit with my—"

"I'm done here." With a jerk of his head, he gestures toward the back door. "Let's go."

I cling to the desk, desperate for an anchor in a chaotic world. "Wait." I can't believe what I'm about to say. "I'll do anything. I'll—I'll have sex with you."

He stares at me like I've lost my mind, and maybe I have, but sex seems like a better solution than death. I'm not ashamed to admit that I've used sex as a bargaining tool throughout my life—the mechanic who replaced my transmission, a former landlord, the cable guy. None of them were as hot as Cash, but I'd been desperate and broke and they'd been more than happy to waive my debts in exchange for sexual favors.

Callie wouldn't approve. Not because she's a prude or because she still loves Cash. They broke up ages ago. She wouldn't approve because she's overprotective of me, and Cash is a definite threat to any woman's sanity.

"You think you're going to repay me with a fuck?" Although his tone is incredulous, he stops then crosses his arms over his chest. "Whores are a dime a dozen in my line of work. I can have a girl in my bed within fifteen minutes who'll do anything I want, and it won't cost me no two hundred grand. What makes your pussy so special?"

No matter how hard I try, I can't come up with one thing to make me special. I'm plain, a little chubby, and my nose is crooked. "I'm desperate."

"All right." The tip of his tongue sweeps across his lower lip, drawing my gaze there. "Gotta say, I've had some great sex but never anything worth two hundred grand. It better be special. How you wanna do this? Against the wall with your panties around your ankles? Or should I bend you over the desk?"

I've never had sex with anyone like Cash Delacorte. Compared to him, the men of my past were boys. My breath comes in short, rapid pants. This is becoming too real for my taste. In my wildest dreams, I never imagined a moment in my life where I'd be exchanging the right to live for sex. Excitement flutters in my belly. This might be wrong, but I'm going to enjoy every minute.

He jerks his chin toward the desk. "Go on. I ain't got all night." When I hesitate, he snakes an arm around my waist. "Yeah. That's what I thought." With a tug, he jerks my body against his. He digs the fingers of his free hand into the nape of my neck and angles my head to the left, aligning my lips with his. The scent of peppermint lingers on his breath. In this position, I can feel the washboard abs beneath his shirt, the strength of his thighs, and the hardness between them.

I *want* him to kiss me. Sure it's twisted, but I can't help longing to see if he tastes as good as he looks. I close my eyes and wait for the brush of his mouth against mine, the slide of his tongue between my parted lips.

I expect roughness, careless groping, and domination. Instead, two velvet lips press against mine. With a little pressure, he parts my lips. His tongue slips inside my mouth, tentative at first then diving deeper. I curl my fingers into his shirt, pulling him close.

"Mmm." A delicious growl rumbles from his throat. The fingers in my hair relinquish their hold before grabbing a handful of my bottom, forcing me onto my toes.

I gasp at the insistent rod of steel behind the fly of his pants. I don't want to like it. He's arrogant and scary and more man than anyone I've ever met. I don't want to like it, but I do. Every kiss before this one fades into oblivion. It's a testament to how fucked up I really am.

"Nah." He releases me as quickly as he grabbed me, keeping a hold on my hip until I regain my balance. Mortification heats my cheeks. Did I misread his signals? Isn't he attracted to me? Am I so inadequate? He shakes his head. Darkness glitters in his eyes. With his little finger, he sweeps the hair from my forehead. "When I fuck you, baby girl, it'll be because you begged me for it. Not because you owe me a debt."

When I fuck you... Which leads me to believe that it's going to happen. Maybe not tonight but someday. I run a hand over my hair in a desperate attempt to collect myself. He's calm and cool, oblivious to the fact that he just rocked my world, while he adjusts the bulge in his pants.

"So here's how this is going to go down. You're going to work for me until you've paid off your debt." He takes the gun from the desk and shoves it into the back of his pants. His somber gaze holds mine. The guy has his emotions on lockdown, that's for sure. I'm both envious and frustrated by his control.

Beneath my fear of Cash and my anger at Calliope for drawing me into this mess is a buzz of excitement. Before he walked through the front door, my life had been boring and predictable. With a threat and a kiss, he's flipped my world upside down. I love a challenge, the thrill of outwitting someone more powerful than me, and Cash Delacorte presents the perfect opportunity to flex my intellectual skills. His granite jaw and soft lips are an added bonus.

A knock on the door reminds me that we aren't alone. Em opens the door and peeks her head around the corner. "Is everything okay? I thought I heard shouting."

"We're fine." My voice is sharp and loud.

"Come on in, Emeline. Join us." The danger in his invitation raises the hackles on the back of my neck. I'm more than happy to play his games, but I won't allow Emeline to be a part of it. "I was just asking your boss here to help me out with that gift for my grandma." He smirks and holds up his phone to display a photo of an emerald pendant. "Think you could make this, Jagger?"

I take the phone, ignoring the sizzle of his fingertips over my skin, and study the example. I have no choice.

If I say no, Em will think I've gone mental, and Cash will never get out of my life. "Um, yeah. Sure." The design is simple, elegant, and classic. Nothing complicated. I can recreate it with little effort. A breath of relief skims over my lips. This seems like a reasonable compromise. I'll make a few pieces of jewelry, using minimal effort, and be done with this man.

"It has to be *exactly* like this. Understand? The highest quality synthetic stone you can find. Nothing but the best for my grandma." He pockets the phone.

I shift into business mode, eager to escape the pull of sexual chemistry between us. "Fine."

"I need it by Tuesday." His gruff voice speaks to my imagination. I'd love to hear his gravelly baritone in my ear after a hot and sweaty session of sex. As if he can read my thoughts, he leans closer. "Can you handle that, Jagger?"

"Yes." My reply floats on a breathy whisper.

"Great." The fabric of his shirt rubs my breast when he brushes past me. Once again, he's a heady combination of charm and charisma. "I'll be in touch."

Emeline and I stare in disbelief at his backside as he exits the store. An indeterminable amount of time passes before she speaks. "Holy freaking hell. What just happened?"

"I know, right?" My throat is dry, my words broken.

"How in hell are you going to make a necklace like that in four days? We're going into the weekend. Where will you get a stone like that?"

"Call Jimmy and see if he can overnight a two-carat

simulated emerald." Four days is a rush, but I have some of the components on hand. If I forgo sleep, I can meet the deadline.

Her eyes widen. "Now?"

"Yes, now." I shove the store phone into her hands. "I'll start working on the setting. I've got those materials on hand." When she doesn't move, I raise my eyebrows. "Emeline?"

"On it." She rolls her lips together. "For the record, that guy might be scary but he's also hot AF."

I give her a playful shove to lighten the mood. I don't want her to suspect anything. "I'm making a pendant for him. How much trouble can that be?"

My personal phone pings with an incoming text from an unknown number. When I open the text, it contains the photo of the pendant and this message: *Looking forward to seeing your work. C.*

He has my phone number. My *private* phone number. I bite my lower lip to hide my unease from Emeline. If he knows my number, what other information does he have? For safety's sake, I'm going to assume the worst. He probably has someone watching me.

"Are you sure you're okay?" Em asks.

"Fine." I shoo her toward the desk. "Stop mothering me."

"Don't hate me for caring." She sticks out her pink tongue then dials Jimmy's number. Her chatter blurs beneath the buzzing in my ears.

The work consumes me to the exclusion of everything else. Nothing gives me more bliss than a challenging project. I love molding metal into graceful shapes, creating beauty using my bare hands. Even the threat of Cash Delacorte can't dampen my enthusiasm. Pride in my craft forces me to do the best work possible. I stay at the store until the early hours of the morning, go home for a few hours of sleep, then return the next day to pick up where I left off. By Monday morning, I'm exhausted but triumphant. The pendant is exquisite. If he's pleased, maybe he'll let me off the hook.

While I'm in the workshop, Emeline fields the occasional customer who comes through the door. Despite her flighty persona, she's a competent salesperson and accountant. We met on a city bus in Philadelphia two years ago and hit it off. She needed to escape the shadow of her overbearing ex-husband while I needed to get away from Kyle. On a whim, we did a Google search for obscure towns, chose the tiny Indiana hamlet as the perfect place to begin our lives over again, and never looked back.

"Are you going to be finished by tomorrow?" she asks on Monday afternoon.

"Done." I hold up the chain, letting the fake emerald pendant spin and wink beneath the overhead lights. "Voila."

"Wow. You're amazing!" The praise heats my face. She shakes her head. Her brown hair bounces over her shoulders. "I don't know how you do it."

"Thanks. I couldn't have done it without you."

"Do you want me to call Cash?" A worried frown

creases her forehead. She twists the pearl ring on her right hand, a familiar sign of her distress.

"I already did." The thought of seeing Cash again stirs butterflies in my belly. "He'll be here tonight."

"And then you'll be done with him, right?" Nudging me aside, she pulls up a stool at my side.

"Of course." Ignoring the implications of her question, I push to another subject. "Are you going out with Tony this weekend?"

"I don't know. Maybe. Do you have any plans?"

"Doubt it. There aren't exactly a lot of choices around here." Less than three thousand people live in this town. The few men my age are married. And, deep down, I'm still not ready for a relationship. "I'll probably download some movies and drink some wine."

"I'm sure Tony has a friend who would love to go out with you. Want him to fix you up?" Her face brightens with hope. "We could double."

"I appreciate the offer, but no." Since beginning my new life, I've gone out of my way to avoid relationships. Thanks to Cash's kiss, however, I've started to wonder if I'm missing out. It would be nice to have dinner with someone other than Emeline or Mr. Mercer.

And maybe there will be *sex.* Goodness, how I miss it.

"Come on. It's time to get back out there." She waggles her eyebrows. The bell over the front door tinkles. Em pops up from the stool. "I'll get it." Thirty seconds later, she's back. "It's for you."

"Is it him?" I frown at the clock over the door. "That was fast."

"No, it's a big, gorgeous blond guy with a beard and enormous guns." To demonstrate, she lifts her arms in a bodybuilder's pose.

"Okay." Using the utmost care, I place the necklace into a velvet box and try not to analyze my disappointment. I should be relieved Cash sent a courier. The less interaction I have with Cash Delacorte, the better for everyone involved.

When I brush past her, she grabs my arm. Concern adds gravity to her usual happy countenance. "Wait. Don't go out there. Let me take it."

"What?"

Her fingers tighten. "I don't know why, but I have a bad feeling about this."

"You're being paranoid."

"Am I?"

"I'll give him the necklace, and we'll never see him again." My words are confident, but inside, I know it's a lie. This is only the beginning.

"Promise?"

"Promise."

Her grip on my arm loosens. I push through the door and trip over an enormous black leather boot. Em crashes into my backside. My gaze travels up a muscular leg covered by faded denim and comes to a halt on a pair of blazing blue eyes.

"Jagger Jones?" The man's voice is deep and

commanding. Full lips and chiseled cheekbones give him a fierce, Viking-like appearance.

For an instant, I consider lying which is ludicrous. Who else would I be? I clear my throat. "Um, yes. That's me."

"You got the necklace?"

"Yes. Here." I thrust the velvet box toward him.

He shakes his head, refusing to take it. "The boss wants you to deliver it."

My heartrate begins to escalate. "I'm afraid that's impossible. I can't leave the store right now." Straightening my shoulders, I give him a polite smile.

With an exhausted sigh, he takes a step closer to me. "That's not the deal."

"If you think I'm going to get in a car with you, you're delusional." I try to maneuver around him, but his buff body blocks my path.

"My instructions are clear. You deliver the merch, or I'm to initiate Plan B." He jerks his head toward the door.

"What's Plan B?" Emeline asks, her voice higher than I've heard it.

He scratches strong fingers through the scruff on his chin. "I'd rather not say, but I can guarantee you won't like it."

"I'm calling the police." Em withdraws her phone, holding it in shaking fingers.

"I wouldn't do that if I were you." The man snatches the phone out of her hand in a lightning fast swipe. "Is she going to be a problem, Jagger?"

I shake my head. "Let's all stay calm. I'm sure we can work this out."

Em, being the fierce protector that she is, tries to wedge between us. "You can't make her go against her will."

"It's okay." Drawing on all my internal strength, I give her a reassuring smile. "I'll drop off the piece, get the money, and be back before bedtime. No worries." Except I won't be paid. I'll be in debt to Jimmy for the fake stones and to Mr. Mercer for the other materials. I look to our visitor for confirmation. "Right, sir?"

"Sounds reasonable," he replies. The tension eases from his shoulders. He sweeps a hand toward the door. "After you, Ms. Jones."

FIVE

Jagger

From the backseat of the Escalade, I recount all the stupid actions that led me to this moment. The deceptions, the forgeries, the money. Too late, I remember the pepper spray in my bedroom closet. I stopped carrying it a few months ago. The lazy pace of small-town living has made me careless. Comfortable. Regrets, however, won't save me. I stare out the tinted window as the cornfields turn into subdivisions then city streets. Each passing mile brings me closer to judgement day and *him*. The handsome devil with bedroom eyes and sinful lips.

"Where are we going?" I ask the driver for the tenth time. He's silent. Not even a flicker of emotion crosses his face. "Can you at least tell me your name?" Maybe I can play on his sympathies. If this meeting heads south, an ally might be nice.

In the rearview mirror, his cool gaze flickers to mine. "Gage."

"Do you work for Cash?"

"Sort of." His answer does little to satisfy my curiosity.

"Did you know my sister Calliope?"

Those intense blue eyes flicker over me, like he's considering whether or not to answer. After a long pause, he nods. "Sure."

"I miss her." The thought of her mischievous smile brings the threat of tears. I swallow down the lump in my throat. If she were here, she'd know how to handle Cash. Then again, if she were here, I wouldn't be in this situation. A twinge of anger curbs my nostalgia. This is partially her fault. If she hadn't stolen the money, Cash would never have entered my life. "Were you friends?"

"No more questions." Gage's gaze snaps back to the road.

Keeping my eyes on the passing scenery, I dig through my purse for anything to defend myself. Tampons, paper clips, ink pen, lipstick, keys—*keys*. I clutch the ring holding my store and house keys in my palm, arranging the blades of the keys between my fingers. It's not a great weapon, but I can probably blind someone. A few seconds is all I need to make my escape.

The car rolls past dilapidated houses with junk cars and boarded windows before coming to a stop in an empty parking lot across from the dock doors of a sketchy warehouse. In the distance, the skyscrapers of Indianapolis stretch toward the darkening sunset. By my calculations, we're somewhere on the east side of the city, an area known for its violence and crime.

"Now what?" My voice cracks. Hiding my growing panic has become a testament to my self control.

"We wait." He shifts in the seat, getting comfortable, and rests an elbow on the door.

I study the unfamiliar street, the alleys, and graffiti-covered store fronts. If an opportunity for escape presents itself, I need to know my options. My best bet is to run like hell and hide. I rub my palms along the tops of my thighs, over and over, finding focus through the repetitive movement. A couple of boys in red bandanas stand on the opposite corner of the intersection, phones to their ears. The shorter kid breaks from his conversation when a Mercedes sedan pulls up next to him. The boy passes a brown paper bag to the driver. The car speeds away. Quick and efficient. Having dated a drug dealer, the process is all too familiar.

Minutes later, a black Range Rover with shiny rims and tinted windows parks next to us. The car door opens, and Cash hops to the ground. His face is barely visible beneath the lowered edge of his knit cap. He flips up the collar of his denim jacket, shoves his hands into his pockets, and nods at Gage. A third car pulls into the lot. This time it's an old, rusty Oldsmobile, the kind my grandmother used to drive. It parks a dozen yards away.

"Get out," Gage says.

With shaking hands, I open the vehicle door. An icy wind blows trash across the faded white paint of parking lines. I shiver. Cash walks forward, his gaze sweeping over the messy bun on the top of my head, my gray hoodie, jeans, and sneakers. On days spent at my workbench, I don't dress up.

"Walk with me?" Although presented in the form of a question, his words demand my compliance. I fall into step beside him. We head toward the Oldsmobile. He's quiet. The silence sets my frayed nerves on edge.

I sneak a peek at Cash through my lashes. The angles of his jaw and cheekbones are cruel but the bow of his lips suggests vulnerability and kisses that deliver all the feels. Threads of auburn shoot through the thickness of his eyebrows. He arches one. Heat burns my face. I drop my gaze to the asphalt and the blades of brown grass shooting through the cracks.

"I have your necklace," I say, hoping to curtail this expedition. I withdraw the box from my purse and hand it to him.

He opens the lid and runs a fingertip over the simulated emerald. "Nice. You did good." His praise heats my insides but doesn't chase away the chill of his brown eyes.

"If we're done here, I'll be on my—"

"Got some business to take care of first." He's so cool, unruffled and calm, as he slides the box into his pocket.

"Is this going to take long?" My voice breaks. I clear my throat for a second attempt. "I mean, I need to get home. Someone's waiting for me."

He ignores me. I stare down the deserted street. One

of the boys on the corner stares back. He gives me a wink, sticks out his tongue, and grabs his crotch. Crude bastard. I snap my attention back to the broken pavement. Cash picks up the pace. I trot to keep up with his long strides.

"Don't you worry about them?" I jerk my chin toward the corner workers, wrapping my arms around my waist.

"Nah." He rolls his shoulders, like he's warding away tension. "They work here because I let them." When we reach the Oldsmobile, he halts and knocks twice on the trunk. The lid pops open to reveal a bound and gagged man.

One glance at the reddish-brown hair, pock-marked skin, and panicked green eyes above the gag makes the world spin. *Jimmy.* Instinctively, I retreat and run into Cash's hard chest.

"Easy, girl." Taking my elbow in his firm grip, he moves me aside. Gage gets out of the Escalade. He shoves a pistol into the back of his jeans then leans against the hood. Jimmy blinks up at us in fearful confusion. Cash rests a hip against the fender, orienting his body to face me. "You two already know each other, so I'm gonna skip the introductions."

It takes a few seconds for the implications of this statement to wash through me. When the truth arrives, it strikes me with painful fury. He knows. He knows. He knows. He knows *everything*. Perspiration dampens my forehead.

"Yeah. I know what you been up to." Cash nods,

like he can understand Jimmy's garbled pleas behind the tape on his lips. "Ain't no use lying about it." He knocks on the side of the car. Two unkempt men climb out of the Olds. They roll up their sleeves to reveal tattooed forearms as they stride toward us. Cash's voice is scratchy but quiet. "I'm gonna need some answers."

This is bad. Oh, so bad. A wave of calm washes over me. Until the breath leaves my body, I have a chance. If I'm going to make a break for it, it needs to be now. I squander precious seconds to scrutinize my adversaries. The two thugs from the Oldsmobile have beer guts and probably couldn't run twenty feet. Cash could be a problem. He's at least a foot taller than I am with long legs. Although he's wearing multiple layers of clothing, the gray hoodie and denim jacket can't hide the body of a man who works out religiously. I might be able to sprint faster than he can, but he'll catch me in a long chase. Gage worries me most. Sometime in the past few minutes, he's shed his jacket. His biceps bulge against the sleeves of his T-shirt as his inked arms cross over his chest. I'll have to act fast and hope that he can't hit a running target.

"Who wants to go first?" Cash lifts an eyebrow, his head turning between me and Jimmy. He rips the duct tape from Jimmy's mouth.

"I had nothing to do with it. It was all her idea. I give her the fake stones. She makes the pieces. I have no idea what she does with them afterward." The words pour out of Jimmy's mouth in a rush. "You know me. I would never cross you, Cash. She came to me. I didn't even want to do it, but she can be very persuasive."

Cash cocks his head, turning his frown in my direction. "Jimmy says you're the culprit, sweet girl. What do you gotta say?"

"I only made the one piece. That's it." I roll my eyes in what I hope is a convincing denial.

"Don't play dumb. It makes you look weak." A muscle ticks in Cash's jaw, but his voice remains even, controlled. "It wasn't one time, Jagger. You and this guy here have been exchanging your fakes for originals all around the city, and you're cutting into my business." His eyes darken to obsidian black. "For a girl, you got some big balls."

"I have no idea what you're talking about." To underscore my innocence, I lift both palms into the air, hoping he'll believe me. As my felonious mother used to say, deny, deny, deny.

"Come on, sweetheart. Do I look like I was born yesterday?" At my continued denial, his eyebrows raise. "Ah, so it's like that. Okay. Let me guess." He crosses his arms over his chest. "You, little girl, case the high-end jewelry stores, copy their pieces, then switch them for the fakes. Jimmy here fences the goods to someone like me and gets a cut of the sale. Very enterprising. I'm impressed."

"You've been selling to *him*?" My blood pressure climbs until spots swim in front of my eyes. I grab my head with both hands. "Jimmy, how could you be so stupid?"

"You never cared what happened to the stuff as long as you got your cut," Jimmy snaps. He squirms against the spare tire, his feet slipping on the worn carpet, and turns his attention to Cash. "She's the mastermind. All I did was move the merch."

"You lied to me, little girl." Ice forms in Cash's dark eyes. "And there's nothing I hate more than a liar."

Gage unfolds his arms and takes a step toward me. I shift from one foot to the other then launch in the opposite direction of the parked cars. The soles of my tennis shoes slap on the pavement in a furious rhythm. I'm not going to die. Not today, and definitely not like this.

"Fuck." Cash's enraged growl echoes in the distance. "Go get her, man."

I put everything I've got into my escape. I run like a crazy woman, pumping my fists and stretching my strides. Footsteps pound behind me. Thank goodness, Gage is wearing heavy leather boots. I need every advantage I can get. Adrenalin burns through my veins. I don't look over my shoulder to check on my pursuer. A childhood spent running from bullies trained me for this moment. At the end of the warehouse, I hang a right and head toward the abandoned lot across the street.

"Come back here, you crazy bitch!" Gage's shout is close enough to send a chill up my spine and a new spike of adrenalin into my limbs.

The cold air ignites in my chest, but I don't let up until I reach the chain link fence of the lot. Digging my fingers into the wires, I scramble over the top. The ground on the other side is hard and unyielding. I land on my hands and knees. Pain shoots up my leg. The warm trickle of blood drips down my calf. Gage grunts as he lands behind me. I sprint forward. His hand tangles in my hair. With one yank, I'm jerked off my feet. I land on my back. The impact knocks the breath out of me.

"What the fuck is wrong with you?" He struggles to capture my flailing arms. "Calm down."

"No," I gasp. By this time, I'm crazed beyond all reason. I haven't been this worked up since my uncle tried to steal my car. The sharp edges of my nails scrape across Gage's face, leaving angry red tracks on his cheek. "Let go." My foot connects with his stomach. It's hard like steel and has no effect on him. He presses a forearm to my throat. I sink my teeth into his wrist.

He hisses at the pain. "Jesus." In two expert motions, he flips me onto my stomach and jabs a knee into my back. With my face in the pavement, I'm rendered helpless. He mutters beneath his breath while he secures cable ties around my wrists. When he's done, he rolls me onto my back and sits cross-legged next to my head. He scrapes a palm over his face. "You're fucking nuts."

"You have no idea." I squirm against the restraints then shout in frustration. "When I get out of this, I'll show you crazy."

To my surprise, he chuckles. "Looking forward to it." Using a bandana from his back pocket, he wipes the sweat from his forehead. Although I'm breathless from the run and too exhausted to continue fighting, he's barely winded. A wry grin gives a handsome light to his rugged features. "For the record, I'm impressed. I never would've guessed you're so fast."

"I ran track in high school." His nod of approval does nothing to soothe my irritation. "You're pretty fast yourself—for a big guy."

"Thanks." Humor curves the corners of his mouth. "I still hold the record for the hundred-yard dash at my high school." He stands and helps me to my feet. "I'd love to sit here and chat some more with you about sports and what not, but the boss is waiting."

His biceps ripple as he throws me over his shoulder. I hang upside down, my face level with the back pockets of his worn blue jeans. His ass is round and taut. The hardness of his shoulder bites into my stomach with each stride. I wriggle to ease the discomfort and am rewarded with a stinging slap on the bottom.

"Settle down," he growls.

When we reach Cash, he dumps me onto my feet. The trunk of the Oldsmobile is closed and eerily quiet. My fear escalates to sheer terror. Cash's brown eyes rove over my face. Using the pad of his thumb, he wipes a smudge of mud from my chin in a tender caress. "Tell me one good reason why I shouldn't throw you in the trunk with your buddy here."

"I'm no good to you dead." I blurt the answer and continue to plead for my life in a torrent of words. "If you kill me, you'll never make your money back. I can make more copies for you. I can work the debt off."

He snorts. "What kind of message will it send my business partners if I let you go?"

My brain races through possible bargaining chips. If he wanted me dead, he would already have done it by now. Every second I can keep him talking is a second longer to make my case.

"If I disappear, people will ask questions. Mr. Mercer depends on me to run the store, and I told Em that I'd be back before bedtime. Her boyfriend is a cop. She'll know something's wrong and call him if I don't come home. They won't give up until they know what happened to me." For good measure, I throw in a wild card. "Calliope will look for me, too."

I'm not sure why, but my final statement causes a hitch in his breath. Storm clouds darken his brow. His gaze flits to the goons. Through some kind of telepathic signal, they nod, get in their car, and speed away, leaving a cloud of blue exhaust in their wake. Cash stands frozen, staring at me, hands in his pockets. The scent of his cologne catches on the spring breeze and wraps around me. His jaw flexes, an outward indication of his inner conflict. My focus locks onto the black ink on his neck. Sexy. *Hot.*

"All right." A long exhale follows. "Take her home."

"You sure about that?" Gage leans toward his boss, a furrow between his thick eyebrows. "Aren't you worried she'll talk?"

"Nah." Cash chucks me beneath the chin. The casual graze of his fingers on my skin sets my heart aflutter in a combination of fear and desire. "She's too smart for that. Aren't you, darlin'?" With an easy shrug, he pivots and walks back to the Range Rover. At the door, he pauses. "I'll be in touch."

Gage drops me at the driveway of my house, cuts the cable ties then disappears into the night. Emeline is sitting in the living room, pretending to watch TV, but I can tell she's been worrying. She runs to meet me. Her gaze takes in my disheveled hair, the rip in my jeans, the drops of blood on my tennis shoes from the cut on my leg. "What happened to you? Are you okay?"

"I tripped over something. It's nothing." I force an easy smile. "You know how clumsy I am."

She nudges me to the sofa. "Sit. I'll get you a glass of water."

"No." I gesture toward the cabinet next to the refrigerator where I keep the whiskey. A night like this calls for something stronger. "Bring the bottle."

She pours an inch of liquor into two glasses and presses one of the tumblers into my palm. I drain it then hold out the glass for a refill. My mind struggles to reconcile everything that happened. The clock over the TV says it's nine o'clock. Have I really only been gone for three hours? It feels like a lifetime.

My phone dings with an incoming text from Cash. "Got a job for you. Going to the club Friday night. Pick you up at seven. Wear something sexy."

My stomach flutters. I quickly delete the text and toss my phone on the sofa. Emeline frowns. "That was him, wasn't it?" I struggle and avoid her gaze, knowing she'll be able to see through my expression. She sighs. "Want to tell me what happened tonight?"

"Not really."

"Did you give him the necklace?"

"I did."

"So you're done with him, right?"

"Not exactly." I take a second gulp of liquor and wait for the mind-numbing relief that never arrives. The night has left me full of uncertainty, but there's one thing I know for sure. Cash Delacorte is in my life, and he's not leaving anytime soon.

SIX

Jagger

With a nervous smile, I meet Emeline's gaze in the mirror. While she was out with Tony, I've been getting ready for whatever Cash has in store for me tonight. "Does this look okay?" I'm wearing a short blue cocktail dress, one that clings to my curves. A good coat of polish hides most of the scuffs on my expensive but worn high heels. Although it's crazy, I want to look good for Cash. I place a hand on my stomach to calm the butterflies inside.

"You look great." She frowns at my reflection. "Where are you going?"

"To the club. With Cash." I hold my breath, waiting for the argument about to unfold.

"After what happened last week? Are you insane?" The high pitch of her voice echoes off the ceiling.

"Probably." Her screeching does nothing to calm my nerves.

"I'd be a shitty friend if I didn't say that going anywhere with this guy is a big mistake."

"Objection noted." Ignoring her accusatory stare, I grab my clutch purse and smooth my hair. On most days, I wear it in a ponytail or bun. Tonight, I'm wearing it in loose waves down my back.

"He's a psychopath." Her mouth forms an O.

"Believe me. If I had a choice, I wouldn't go." For the last twenty-four hours, I've wracked my brain for an exit strategy and come up with nothing. Cash is smart and scary and too powerful to avoid. Meanwhile, I'm the idiot who blew all his money on designer dresses and bad investments.

Her footsteps shadow mine into the hallway, persistent to the end. "You moved here to get away from guys like him."

"This is different." Since I don't know how to explain, I don't even try. She knows about the problems I had with Kyle. At his memory, I touch the scar above my left eyebrow, the one he gave me after an argument over something insignificant. Cash has one there, too. It's something we have in common, and I have to wonder who marked him.

"How? How is it different?" With both hands on her hips, she blocks the front door. "He's another bad boy from the wrong side of the tracks."

"Maybe." I can't argue with her logic.

"He's here." She draws aside the curtains of the living room window. "And he's coming to the door. At least he's a gentleman."

"Great. Wish me luck." Nervous butterflies flit in my stomach. I didn't expect him to come to the door.

"Why do you need luck?" Lines of concern furrow her forehead. "Say the word, and I'll go out there and tell him you're sick or something."

"Don't be ridiculous." But I *am* sick—sick with worry, sick with nerves, sick with anticipation. I have no idea what he has in store for me tonight, but I'm pretty sure it's going to end with sex. Not because he likes me, but because he owns me, and I owe him. My panties dampen at the thought of his heavy body on top of me. I fan my face with my hands to keep the ensuing heat flash from ruining my makeup.

The doorbell rings. Our eyes meet. She blocks the door—gives me a final, pleading look. My insides twist into knots. Oh God. I'm not ready for this. Not by a long shot. When I raise my eyebrows, she steps aside. I open the door slowly. Cash stands on the front steps. My heart skips a beat. His dark eyes sweep over me, from head to toe and back up again. I sweep a hand to the side, inviting him into the foyer.

"You look great, little girl. I could eat you up." His praise sends a flush of heat into my cheeks. Wait. No. This isn't a date. He's a dick and a criminal. Inwardly, I roll my eyes at my behavior. Later, I'll have to dissect all the ways my attraction to him is inappropriate and unhealthy. For the moment, I need to survive.

"Thanks. You look nice, too." I'm not sure what kind of game he's playing, but I can be civil. And it isn't a lie. Beneath his black leather jacket, he's wearing a starched black dress shirt—the expensive kind—and charcoal dress pants. He's the kind of guy to make me look twice then look again for good measure.

He extends one of two roses to me. "For you."

"Thanks." I lift the crimson petals to my nose and inhale the sweet scent while trying to corral my thoughts. Does *he* think this is a date? Did I miss something? I'm so confused. A thorns pricks my finger. I hiss at the sting. The pain reminds me to separate Cash's pretty words from his deceptive actions.

"And one for your friend." He hands the second rose to Emeline. She gapes at him before gingerly taking it.

"Thanks." Her gaze slides over to me. Her forehead puckers in confusion. "What club are you guys going to?"

I glance back to Cash who's chill and casual, his tall body overpowering the small entryway of my house. He shrugs. "It's private. Very exclusive. Don't wait up." Taking my elbow, he guides me toward the door. "Don't worry. I'll take care of her."

Em stands next to the door, arms crossed over her chest. "I'll have my phone at my side. If you need me, call me, Jag." With narrowed eyes, she watches as Cash places a hand on the small of my back and ushers me outside.

A blast of cold air races across my bare legs. I shiver. He gives me an intense sideways glance. "Where's your coat, baby girl?"

"I—I don't have one that matches." My teeth chatter, making my words stilted. I have a puffy coat for winter and a windbreaker for spring. Until now, I never needed more. "I'll be fine."

Wordlessly, he shrugs out of his jacket and drapes it around my shoulders. The lining is still warm with his body heat and smells like him—clean, sharp, and musky. He opens the door behind the driver of the Escalade. Three men are inside. Two goons in front. Gage in the back. The hoods of their sweatshirts are pulled over their heads. None of them look at me. I balk. *Three* men? Cash gives me a little shove. "Get in."

I go because I have no choice and because I'm curious to see where the night takes us. He slides into the backseat next to me and shuts the door. He pats the driver's headrest, signaling for us to leave. Gage hugs his side of the car, staring out the window into the darkness. Cash spreads his knees wide. The hard length of his thigh presses against mine. I can feel his muscles through the fabric of his trousers. Every time he shifts, an electric thrill races up my leg.

"Where are we going?" I ask.

Cash turns his attention to the window. "You'll know when we get there." The smooth yet scratchy texture of his voice makes my blood sing with desire and fear.

I focus on the road, searching for clues about our destination. It's the not knowing that bothers me. I have no idea what he has in store for me tonight. A little time to prepare would have been nice. Tension thickens the air. No one speaks. The silence roars in my ears. To release some of my anxiety, I bob my leg. Cash places a hand on my knee, squeezes until I stop, and leaves it there. My body sizzles beneath his command. His touch travels all the way to my center. I squeeze my legs together to ease the throbbing inside my panties. I want his hands on me, inside me, teasing, tickling, and groping.

After an endless forty-five minutes, the Escalade turns through a wrought iron gate and onto a private drive. In the darkness, I can make out a manicured landscape with decorative ponds and trees. Rows of expensive cars line the pavement. We roll to a stop in front of a castle-like mansion. The sign above the door says we're at Hellwater Hills Country Club. I've heard of this place. It's the most exclusive country club in the state, the playground of congressmen, professional sports players, and various other rich people.

"When you said we were going to a club, I thought you meant a bar," I say.

"This is a club," Cash replies. The men laugh. My face heats with embarrassment. I hate being laughed at almost as much as I hate being blackmailed.

"You should've told me," I snap. "I would've worn something more appropriate." My short dress seems a little too daring for a conservative place like this.

"That dress looks good on you." A smirk curls the corners of his mouth. "Can't help thinking you'd look a whole lot better out of it, though."

Outwardly, I ignore his flirtatious compliment. Mostly because I have no idea whether he's serious or teasing. That's the thing about Cash. He's unreadable.

Inside, my temperature rises a few degrees because I want his words to be true. I shift my attention back to the elegant manor. "They're going to know I don't belong here." With a worried scowl, I tug the hem of the dress, trying to make it longer.

"Stop. You've got gorgeous legs. You'll be fine." He dismisses my worries with a wave of his hand. "Here's what's about to go down. Are you listening, Jagger? I'm only gonna say this once." His fingers tighten on my knee, forcing my attention to that part of my anatomy again.

"Yes." A strange flutter awakens in my lower belly. I bet those fingers know their way around a woman's body.

"All right. You're going to go inside and find a man named Hubert Spillman. Short dude, bald head, glasses. Got a purple birthmark on his forehead. You'll know him when you see him." He speaks casually, like we're discussing the weather over coffee. "Give him this." From the depths of his shirt pocket, he withdraws a flash drive and tucks it into my cleavage. Gooseflesh pebbles along my skin at the brush of his fingertips over my breast. My nipples jut against the filmy fabric, begging for his attention. "He's going to give you an envelope. You bring it back to me." He snaps his fingers. "In. Out. Back in ten minutes."

"That's it?" I ask, confused by the simplicity of the task. "If it's so easy, why don't you do it?"

"Let's just say the people inside aren't a fan of my kind." His gaze roves over my body, lingering on my curves. "But you—you've got that sweet, good girl look." He extends an open palm. "Give me your phone."

"Why?" Every fiber of my being wants to rebel against his authority. Resentment for his control over my life leaves a bitter taste in my mouth.

"Damn, why you gotta question everything, girl? Just give it to me."

At his growing impatience, I unsnap the clutch, dig out my phone and slap it into his palm. I bite my lower lip knowing this is all the explanation I'm going to get. He opens the car door, exits, and extends a hand to help me out. I stand next to the vehicle on wobbly legs— partly from nerves and partly from his nearness. He drags his jacket from my shoulders and tosses it inside the Escalade. With a nod toward the entrance, he says, "Go on now."

SEVEN

Jagger

My high heels click on the slate tiles of the entryway. The sound echoes up to the coffered ceilings. An enormous crystal chandelier casts prisms of light on the burled walnut paneling. It takes all of my composure to keep from gawking at the ornate furnishings, the original oil paintings, and the heavy velvet drapes. Everything is so elegant. I feel like a Shetland pony in a stable meant for Thoroughbreds.

"Miss? May I help you?" a male voice calls to me as I head toward the largest set of double doors.

After a deep, calming breath, I turn to face him, wearing my most pleasant expression. The badge fastened to the lapel of his suit marks him as the club manager. "Um, no. Thank you. I know where I'm going." I gesture toward the double doors where the faint hum of voices and laughter emanates.

"May I see your membership card?" The man

extends a hand, waiting expectantly. "Or your invitation?"

"Oh, I'm not a member. I'm here to meet—" My mind goes blank. *Crap!* What was the man's name? Speakman? Spellman? "I'm here to meet Mr. Spillman."

"Senior or Junior?"

There's more than one? I squelch the urge to cuss. Here goes nothing. "Senior."

"Wait here, please." The young man pivots on his heel and strides down a darkened corridor.

The minute he's out of earshot, I sprint toward the ballroom. Two women walk out of the powder room, and I almost bump shoulders with one of them. Both are tall and slender in floor-length gowns, their hair swept into sleek chignons. One of them stops in front of me. I don't know why the hell I get myself into these situations. A spike of adrenalin turns my fear into an intoxicating buzz. I'm actually enjoying this.

"That's a pretty dress." The blonde's unnaturally plump lips stretch into a smile, but her forehead remains smooth and unwrinkled. "Valentino?"

"Thank you and yes." I trace a fingertip along the feather-and-sequin trim on the shoulders. The four-figure price tag had been hard to swallow, but it fits perfectly. It's the most expensive dress I ever bought. Back then, I had money to burn. *Cash's money,* I remind myself.

"Last season, though, right?" The smile on her ruby red lips is perfect yet poisonous.

"Like your earrings?" I ask, mimicking her smirk.

The small, diamond and pearl bobs were showcased at a few trade shows the previous year. Things like that don't matter to me, but the flare of her nostrils suggests I've landed a successful blow to her ego.

"My husband gave them to me as a gift." A blush of mortification brightens her cheeks.

"Have we met?" The second woman peers at me a little too closely. Her attention lingers on my diamond earrings and glittering tennis bracelet. The pieces I borrowed from the store for tonight. "Are you Ambrose Taylor's niece?"

"Yes. Yes, I am." Thank goodness, I've always been able to think on my feet. My core temperature raises to inferno level. How long before one of these women realizes that I'm an imposter and has me tossed out the door? The best option is to get the hell out of here. "I'm so sorry. I'm really late. But I'll find you later, and we can have a chat." I flash a blinding smile then dash in the opposite direction before she can ask more questions.

A set of side doors leads me into the ballroom. The soothing refrains of a string quartet float on the night air. Beyond the champagne fountain, a two-story wall of windows overlooks the lake. I pause to reflect on the grandeur before scanning the sea of tuxedos and designer gowns for Hubert Spillman. The opulence overwhelms the trailer park girl inside me. So this is what it's like to be rich and privileged. Skirting the edges of the dance floor, I maneuver my way through the crowd to the opposite side of the room.

Hubert is there, surrounded by a circle of men. I recognize the half-moon birthmark on his shiny bald head. Must be Hubert Senior. My lungs ache, and I'm suddenly dizzy, like there isn't enough air in the room. I shove my nervousness aside and stride toward him. I hover at his elbow until he notices me.

"Can I help you?" He glances up at me, annoyed by the interruption. Even though I'm only five-foot-six, my heels make me a few inches taller than he is.

"I'm so sorry to intrude, Mr. Spillman. Could I speak with you for a minute?" Even though I'm an anxious wreck, my voice is confident.

"Not now. I'm busy." His rude dismissal ruffles my calm. I just want this to be over.

"Cash sent me."

The color drains from his face. With a hand on my elbow, he escorts me through the nearest door and into a dark library. He locks the door, flips on the lights, and turns to face me with an outstretched hand. "Do you have it? Give it to me."

"Um, yes." I dig the flash drive from my cleavage and drop it into his palm. He walks over to the desk, powers on the computer, and inserts the device. From where I'm standing, I have a clear view of the monitor. With a few clicks of the mouse, he calls up a dozen photos—none of them flattering. All of them explicit. Hubert is naked, his tiny penis in the mouth of a younger man. They both seem to be enjoying them-selves. Me—not so much.

"You're going to burn in hell for this." The color of

his birthmark darkens from purple to a deep shade of eggplant. Perspiration breaks out on his forehead. He mops the sweat from his face with a handkerchief. His chest rises and falls with his labored breathing.

"Are you okay?" I ask.

"Of course not." Spittle flies from his lips. "If my wife finds out about Pierre, she'll take everything I own."

"Look. I just need the envelope, and I'll get out of here." I can't feel sorry for a man who cheats on his wife.

"Ahh." One of his chubby hands clutches the placket of his shirt. His head falls face first onto the keyboard.

"Oh, shit." I give his shoulder a tentative shake. "Mr. Spillman?" He doesn't respond.

"Hubert? Oh, there you are." A tall, elegant woman glides into the library from a second entrance. Her gaze bounces from me to the slumped figure behind the desk. "What's going on here? Who are you?"

"Um, I wandered in here by mistake. I was trying to find the ladies room, and I saw him slumped over the computer." Hubert's head is pressing on the scroll buttons. The disgusting photos flash over the screen. In a moment of clarity, I power down the monitor, but his heavy body blocks access to the USB port. "I think he's having a heart attack." Nothing could've prepared me for a situation like this. "Mr. Spillman?"

"Oh my God. I'm his wife. Call 9-1-1." She rushes to his side and presses two fingers on his throat. "I can't find his pulse. Hubert!"

With shaking hands, I grab the phone on the desk and dial the number while she yanks off his tie and unbuttons his shirt. The operator answers on the fourth ring. "9-1-1. What is your emergency?"

I rattle off the information. Meanwhile, a few people have wandered in from the hall, drawn by the woman's shrieks. Someone yells for a doctor. There's no way to retrieve the flash drive without causing a major disruption. I set the phone receiver on the desk then sprint toward the nearest exit. I run through the kitchen, to the bewilderment of the chef and his assistants, and out the service entrance on the backside of the building. By the time I reach the Escalade, I'm out of breath.

"Did you get it?" Cash catches me by the arm, hauls me toward the backseat. "Where's the payment?"

"No. There were—complications." I don't want to get into the car with him, but at this point, it seems like my only option. "Unless you want to talk to the police, we need to go. Now."

EIGHT

Jagger

A s we exit the gates of Hellwater Country Club, an ambulance approaches in the oncoming lane of the highway. Cash scrapes a hand over his face. He's pale beneath his tan, sensual lips flattened into a thin line. "You wanna tell me what happened in there?"

"He had a heart attack." The tips of my fingers are numb. Probably shock. "I think he's dead. I've never seen someone die before."

"Shit." He drapes his jacket around my shoulders, tugging the edges tight around me, then shoves back in the seat to stare out the window. "Are you okay?"

"Yes."

"Did you at least bring back the thumb drive?"

"Someone walked in. There were too many people. I barely made it out of there." I pull the edges of the jacket snuggly about my chest, wishing the soft leather would swallow me up, unable to drive away the chill of what had happened.

"I gave you one simple task, and you couldn't even get that right." He sighs. "Not good, little girl. Not good."

"What did you expect?" Too many emotions tumble around inside me. Fear, uncertainty, anger. My temper makes a rare appearance. "I'm not a criminal."

"Told you this was a bad idea." Gage lowers the hood of his sweatshirt and runs a hand through his dark blond hair. "Now what?"

"I don't know, Gage." The steel edge of Cash's words sends an ominous ripple down my spine.

"Can I go home now?" I ask. All I want is to feel the warmth and security of my own bed and try to forget this night ever happened.

"No. You cannot go home now. Not until we figure this out." His words are clipped, angry. Even the darkness can't hide the fury in his glare. I shrink into the seat and try not to think about how this might end. He taps the driver's headrest. "You know where to go."

Our next stop is an alley. The driver parks between two trash bins. Cash weaves his fingers through mine and escorts me through a rear entrance into the building. Gage follows on my heels, perhaps to keep me from bolting again. Rock music vibrates through the walls. After navigating a labyrinth of hallways, we emerge next to the band and their stage.

A mass of people clog the dance floor. They bob and

sway in unison. Laser lights cut through the darkness. My chest pounds with each beat of the bass drum. Cash tightens his grip on my hand and weaves his way through the crowd to the only empty table in the place. A red velvet half-moon sofa borders one side.

"Sit." Cash sweeps a hand toward the sofa. I sit on the end. He lifts an eyebrow, prompting me to scoot around to the center. He claims the place next to me. His thigh presses against mine. Although he hasn't said a word, I feel like he's making a statement, claiming me.

Gage takes a seat on my left, bracketing me between his large body and Cash's more athletic one. The other men pull up chairs across from us. We're joined by several thin, lovely women in dresses shorter than mine. A bright-eyed blonde trails her fingers along Gage's chest. He shoves her hand away. She takes the rejection in stride and moves to one of the other men.

"What is this place?" I ask.

"Notorious. My club." He stretches an arm along the back of the sofa. The sleeve of his shirt brushes the nape of my neck. As usual, my body hums at his slightest touch. His palm rests on my knee. When he squeezes my leg, an electric pulse charges up my thigh. "What are you drinking? Beer? Wine? Champagne? Anything you want." His tone has changed from angry to casual.

I clear my throat, hoping he hasn't noticed the way his touch affects me. "A whiskey sour?"

"You got it." His hand leaves my leg, and I miss it the moment it's gone.

Gage raises a hand, motioning for a waitress. The nearest girl approaches. She's wearing tiny black shorts and a mid-riff baring black T-shirt with "Notorious" printed across her ample breasts. A wide smile stretches her glossy lips. "Hey, guys. Cash." She tosses her long hair over a shoulder. "What can I get for you? The usual?"

"Yeah. And a whiskey sour for my lady." Cash smiles back at her. I shiver at his possessive label.

"You got it, babe." She winks and sashays toward the bar, putting an obvious extra swing into her hips.

I don't like this woman. I don't like her perky D-cup tits, her tiny waist, or the way her eyes rake over Cash. Which is ridiculous. I huff and cross my arms over my chest. As far as boyfriend's go, Cash would make the worst of the worst. He's arrogant, criminal, and…I'm unable to finish the thought because his hand lands on my leg again. Higher up this time and slides between my thighs. On instinct, I slam my legs together, trapping his fingers next to my panties. He chuckles. Realizing my mistake, I force my muscles to relax, but his hand stays where it is.

The heavy beat of the music thumps in my chest. I scan the dance floor, curious about the mix of people. Men in business suits. Bearded guys in leather jackets. Women in short dresses. Tattooed girls with vibrant hair and piercings. They all carry an edge of danger about them.

"Anything else?" The waitress returns with our

drinks. Her gaze flits from Cash to me then back to him, dismissing me as inconsequential. "Anything at all?" Her mouth curls upward in a mischievous smirk. "You haven't been over in a while. I've missed you."

Cash's hand tightens on my thigh, like he can read my mind and is reprimanding me for my jealous thoughts. How could he possibly know? I've got to get my emotions on lockdown before he can use my insane attraction to him as a weapon. I lift my chin and try to inch away, but his grip on my leg remains firm and unyielding, holding me in place.

He strokes the bottom of his chin with the backs of his fingers. "Not tonight, babe. I've got my hands full."

"Okay." The smile slips from her face. "Let me know if you change your mind." She pivots in the direction of the bar. The line of her shoulders droops a little.

"Is that your girlfriend?" I can't help asking.

"Not your business," he replies.

"Just making conversation." His refusal to answer leaves my curiosity unsatisfied. Sex oozes from every inch of his long, lean body. A man like him probably has a different woman in his bed every night. This thought proves more unsettling than the previous ones. His fingers drum a tattoo on the inside of my leg. The tickle of his fingertips brings my nipples to tight points. He's such a dick, but my body wants him anyway.

The band goes on a break. The dance floor clears giving me a better view of the place. Metal pub tables and chairs circle the perimeter. Connecting rooms hold pool tables and dartboards. Overhead, exposed pipes crisscross the rooms.

Cash jerks his chin toward the far side of the room. "You see that? " Gage's gaze turns in the same direction.

Five men cross the dance floor, heading in our direction—two in front, three trailing behind. They're wearing identical denim jackets with a unique bird stitched onto the pocket in a pattern that I've seen somewhere else. On Cash's neck. The leader is short and stocky, with a full beard and moustache. His laser-sharp gaze is focused on us. This man is scary, but it's the guy in back who has my attention. The tilt of his head, the way one shoulder is slightly lower than the other, the brown shaggy hair.

The ringing in my ears overtakes the noises in the club. I tug at the neckline of my dress. The clinging fabric is suffocating me. I need to get out of here. Cash tightens his grip on my leg. Escape isn't possible. I'm trapped between two powerful men.

Gage shifts the girl in his lap to one side. "Time to go, sweetheart." She rises obediently and makes her way back to the bar. He leans over. Says something unintelligible to the man next to him. Everyone gets up from the table. Everyone but Cash, Gage, and me.

"Don't say a word," Cash warns. "If anything happens, you stick with Gage. Understand?"

"Yes." The single syllable is all I can muster. My throat constricts in a wave of nervous anxiety. Is he expecting trouble? I'm too rattled to process what's going on.

The group arrives at the table. The leader lifts his chin, staring down at us with obvious disdain. "It's been a long time, Delacorte."

"Not long enough," Cash replies. Although his demeanor remains unchanged, tension hums through his leg and into mine.

Gage leans forward, his hands beneath the table. "You're not welcome here, Reaper."

The man laughs. It's a rattling, disconcerting sound that scrapes over my nerves "Good to see you, too, my friend." His gaze drifts from Gage to me. Bold, eyes rake over my face, my breasts. The tip of his tongue slides over his bottom lip. The remains of my last meal sour in the pit of my stomach. "Who's your friend?"

"She's mine and that's all you need to know." Cash draws me closer. In this bizarre situation, I'm happy to belong to Cash. I go to his side willingly because the man behind Reaper is Kyle, and he's more frightening to me than Cash could ever be.

"What's your name, darlin'?" His smile reveals a gold cap on one of his front teeth.

"You don't talk to her. You don't look at her. You don't touch her." The cold fury in Cash's voice sends a chill down my spine. "If you see her on the street, you cross to the opposite side. Understand me?"

"She's pretty." Reaper's eyes are flat, misty, and gray like a foggy morning. "I wonder if she tastes as sweet as Chelle did."

Chelle? I glance at Cash for a clue to this woman's identity. Was she his lover? A friend? A business associate?

The muscles in Cash's body tighten. His fury seeps through his clothes and into my side, sending a shiver down my back. "You're in my house now." Cash's fingers dig into my leg. The noise in the bar has fallen into complete silence. All eyes are on us. "If you want to live, state your business and get out."

Reaper scratches his chin with dirty fingernails. "I'm here because the FBI have been sniffing around our business. You wouldn't know anything about that, would you?"

"I try to keep my distance from the feds." The line of Cash's jaw becomes sharper. "And I'm not a rat."

"Ah, well—" Reaper shrugs. "I'm sure I don't need to remind you, but you took an oath of allegiance to us. If you know something, you're honor bound to report it."

"I don't owe you shit. I left the DOR years ago." Even though Cash's voice is quiet, his rage is palpable. "I paid the price for my defection a million times over."

"No one gets out. You know that." Reaper starts to turn then halts. His gaze lands on me once more. "What about you? Wanna come with me? I can offer you so much more than this loser."

"No, thank you." I lean into Cash's shoulder, wishing I could evaporate into thin air.

For the first time, Kyle's gaze lands on mine. Recognition flares in his gaze. He cocks his head to one side, eyes narrowing. One corner of his mouth tugs upward. A mixture of fear and hatred solidify in my blood. He shouldn't be here. He should be in prison. Did he get parole? An early release? I was a fool to think I was safe from him.

"No? Well, suit yourself." Reaper shrugs. "I've got plenty of whores. One more would be an inconvenience."

Gage launches out of his chair, tackling Reaper and knocking him to the floor. Cash jumps to his feet like he's going to join in. I cling to his bicep. He's an island of safety in this sea of chaos. My touch seems to snap him out of his daze. His arm wraps around my shoulders. A dozen of Cash's friends come forward, blocking Kyle and the others from interference. Gage and Reaper grapple, tipping over a chair in the process. After a suspenseful minute, Gage drags Reaper to his feet. "If you ever come in here again, I'll gut you like a fish."

"Go ahead." Reaper yanks away from Gage's grasp then shifts his shoulders beneath his jacket. Amusement glints in his gaze. "And maybe I'll tell you how your beloved Chelle begged for her life, right up to the very last breath in her delicious body." Gage roars, his lips white with fury.

Before he can launch a second attack, Cash raises a hand, bringing the pandemonium to a stop. "Enough." He nods toward the men who came with us in the Escalade. "Escort these guys outta here."

Reaper and his gang are booted out the front door. I stare after Kyle until his backside disappears. Silence blankets the room. Cash shoves a trembling hand through his hair then exhales a long breath. "Who the fuck let them through the door?" Blank stares answer his inquiry. He clears his throat, turns to his bouncers, and speaks in his quiet tone. "Find out how this happened."

Gage straightens his clothing. A wild light glows in his blue eyes, like he's high on adrenalin. "That son of a bitch needs to die." The ragged emotion in his voice speaks to my heart. He wears his pain on his face. I want to hug him, but my feet are rooted to the floor.

Cash grabs Gage by the shoulders, forcing him to meet his gaze. "He's trying to get under your skin. *All* of them will pay for what they did to Chelle. Every last one. I promise you." The stare between the two men teems with intensity. "Pull it together. We have a plan. Patience wins this game."

"You're right." Gage shakes his head, clearing his thoughts, and straightens his shoulders. "It's just taking too damn long."

"I know." Cash's tone is soft and introspective. Gage glances away, his blue eyes glittering with something that might be tears.

The staff works to right the tables and chairs. At Cash's nod, the band starts, and the dancers return to the floor. The flirty waitress delivers new cocktails, but Cash waves them away.

"Who is Chelle?" I ask. Whoever she is, she's had a

profound effect on these two men. Seeing their emotions gives me a new perspective on their lives. Although they're intimidating, they also have feelings. My chest aches with empathy for their loss.

"Not now." The hard line of Cash's jaw serves as a warning to keep my mouth shut. He grips my elbow. "Let's get out of here."

The imminent threat of danger has ended, but my anxiety over Kyle returns. I haven't seen him since his trial and conviction. The memory of what he did to me is fresh and raw. I touch the scar above my eyebrow, reliving the pain and horror of his fists. He's here. In my world. Too close for comfort. I'll never be safe from him.

"I need to visit the restroom," I say, forcing my voice to remain calm, shoving my anxiety deep into a shadowy corner of my soul.

Cash's gaze narrows as he searches my face. "Five minutes. Hurry."

I tug down the hem of my dress and scurry toward the hall. Inside the bathroom, I run cold water over my wrists, rest my hands on the edge of the sink, and stare into the mirror. This is a nightmare. I'm about ten minutes from losing my shit. My reflection shows a girl with troubled dark eyes and the pallor of fear beneath her skin. I grab a paper towel and dry my hands. "Suck it up, Jag. You can do this," I mutter to myself.

"You still talk to yourself." The familiar voice comes from the stall to my left.

My throat tightens, making it hard to swallow. I lift

my eyes to see Kyle leaning against the stall door, watching me. Time screeches to a halt. The door is a few paces away. I run toward it, but he gets there before me and blocks my escape with an arm. I back up until I hit the sink. My gaze darts around the room, looking for anything to use as a weapon.

"I got an early release, thanks to Reaper. The Disciples of Rage are great friends to have." His stare travels up and down the length of my body. Although he hasn't touched me, the memory of his hands on me churns my stomach. "You look good, Jag."

"You look terrible." He's lost weight. Acne scars pit his skin. He's got a tribal tattoo on his neck, a teardrop below the corner of his eye, a naked woman on his forearm. On Cash, the artwork is sexy. Kyle's ink is blurry and frightening. I grip the edge of the sink until my knuckles ache. "I have a restraining order."

His laughter lifts the tiny hairs on the nape of my neck. "I belong to the DOR. Restraining orders don't mean shit to me."

With each word, he advances a step. As the gap closes between us, flashes of that fateful night replay through my head. The sensation of falling. Shards of pain. A boot in my ribs. The scream of an ambulance siren.

"Stay away from me." I assume a defensive stance, fists in front of me, weight balanced to evade his attack. Although I haven't practiced in a while, the basics of self-defense are burned into my brain.

"Is that any way to—" He never gets a chance to finish the sentence. The bathroom door flies open and bounces off the wall behind it. Cash rockets into the room, his movements blurred by speed. His hand closes around Kyle's throat. He slams the smaller man against the nearest stall, breaking the door off its hinges.

"Go." Cash jerks his head at me. "Gage is waiting outside."

I don't wait around. I sprint past the men and through the door. Gage grabs my arm, hustles me out the rear entrance and into the waiting Escalade. My heart bangs against my ribs. I press a hand to my sternum to ease the pain. A few minutes later, Cash climbs into the vehicle, taps the headrest, and leans back against the seat.

"Wanna tell me what that was about?" he asks, turning his enigmatic gaze to me.

"Just a misunderstanding." I lift my chin and meet his stare. The less he knows about my past, the better.

"Did he hurt you?" His voice is soft and intimate, meant for my ears alone. He reaches out to sweep my hair away from my face, dragging warm fingertips over my cheek and along my jaw, tipping my chin upward.

"No. I'm fine. He just scared me." Despite my vow to remain stoic, my lips tremble. I don't want to think what might have happened if Cash hadn't interrupted Kyle.

"Are you sure?" The pad of his thumb slides over my bottom lip. His gaze locks onto my mouth, hangs there. "If anyone bothers you, I'll take care of them. You're with us now, and we protect our own. Understand?"

The sincerity of his statement arouses conflicting emotions—gratitude, desire, anxiety. He wraps an around my shoulders and pulls me into his chest, adding to my confusion. The scent of his cologne teases my nose. I exhale and curl my fingers into the lapels of his jacket. He's warm, safe, and strong. The hardness of his chest provides refuge when I haven't felt safe in a very long time.

"Yes." I nod and blink up at him. Without warning, his lips are on mine. Firm yet soft, tender but strong. I melt into his kiss, instinctively moving closer. Too soon, he pulls away, clearing his throat like he's remembering who we are to each other. I shake my head. "You threaten my life but offer to protect me? You're making crazy."

A rare smile turns up his mouth. He taps my nose with a fingertip. "Back atcha, little girl."

"Can I please go home now?" I'm exhausted. I want to go home, crawl into my bed, and rehash the craziness of this night.

"Not yet. We still need to figure out how you're going to repay me for Mr. Spillman." He ends the conversation by turning his face toward the window.

Thirty minutes later, we pull into the circular drive of an elegant, modern mansion, and I'm herded through tall, glass doors into the foyer. Cash tosses his keys onto a table. I flinch at the crash of metal on metal. The men disperse throughout the house, leaving us alone.

Everything is blindingly white—the furnishings, the walls, the floors. In front of me are three stories of windows that overlook a lake. Cash jogs down five steps into the living room. I stand alone in the center of the white marble floor, unable to move. Too terrified to run. He turns around and motions for me to follow. "Come on."

I trail along behind him, up a sweeping staircase to the third floor. He swings open the doors into a massive master suite. With the flick of a remote control, the gas logs in the fireplace leap to life. He sinks into the sofa, stretches an arm along the back, and rests an ankle on the opposite knee. His dark clothing and tattoos contrast with the pristine simplicity of the house. I can think of only one reason why he's brought me here, and the notion both thrills and terrifies me.

"Whose house is this?" I halt in the middle of the room, between the bed and the sofa, and wrap my arms around my waist.

"Mine." He lifts an eyebrow. "Surprised?"

"I am." In my imagination, he lived in a dingy apartment with smoke-stained walls and worn furnishings. Not a palatial estate in the swankiest location in Indiana. Everything about this man contradicts or exceeds my expectations.

"Yeah, well, just 'cause I look like a thug, don't mean I live like one." As he speaks, he unbuttons his cuffs and rolls them up, exposing his lean forearms and the ink covering them.

"I didn't mean to offend you. I just—I thought you lived in Chicago."

"I do, but I'm looking to expand my business, and I needed somewhere to crash while I'm here." He twirls a finger through the air. "You know, diversification and all that."

We fall silent. He studies me, seemingly comfortable with the quiet. Unable to withstand his scrutiny, I walk over to the window. This has to be Geist Lake, home to the ultra-rich. One seamless pane of glass provides a panoramic view of the water. Several terraces hold a swimming pool, jacuzzi, and firepit. At the bottom of the landscaped lawn, recessed lights illuminate a boathouse and dock. Several more expensive homes edge the opposite shore. All of them magnificent. All of them lit up like national monuments.

On the table next to the window sits a sculpted butterfly. It's an amalgamation of stained glass, porcelain, and gold leaf. An odd item for a masculine man like Cash to have in his bedroom. I pick it up. I've dealt with original crafts long enough to recognize the artist's eye for detail. At the base, the black-and-white portrait of a dark-eyed girl smiles up at me. "This is amazing. Who made it?"

"Chelle." Cash's voice cracks. "Beautiful, isn't it?" His breath puffs against the back of my neck. I had no idea he had left the couch. For such a tall man, he moves with the stealth of a cat. I'm reminded of the way he sprinted into the bathroom and collared Kyle. Quiet. Without warning. Predatory. My nerves are soothed by a wave of desire.

"Yes." My body sizzles at his nearness. "She's very talented.

He removes the sculpture from my hands and returns it to the table. "How do you like the view?" The blatant change of topic persuades me to set aside my curiosity for another day.

"It's lovely. But I'm sure you didn't bring me here to admire your home."

"You know why you're here." He blows softly on my nape. The tips of my breasts sting with arousal.

"I'm sorry about tonight. About your flash drive." Having him so near does crazy things to my insides. A war rages between my head and my body. Maybe I can play on his attraction to buy some time. I only need a few minutes to find the nearest exit then I can call Em to pick me up. Except he still has my phone. *Crap.*

"Yeah, shame about that." His heavy sigh tickles my earlobe. "By my calculations, you now owe me two hundred and fifty thousand dollars."

"I'll never be able to pay you back when you keep adding to the debt."

"Plus interest. Let's say twenty-five percent."

"That's not fair."

"Nothing about this world is." The deep growl of his voice reverberates throughout my body. He hasn't touched me, but I can feel him everywhere. In my head, in my breasts, between my legs. Without warning, he retreats to the sofa. He spreads his arms wide across the backrest. "I'm open to suggestions."

"Haven't we been down this road before?" I snap. "I have nothing. You're wasting your time with me."

His broad chest lifts and falls with a heavy breath. He drums his fingers on the back of the sofa. "That bracelet you're wearing. Those are diamonds, right? And the earrings?"

"I—I borrowed them from work." I'd hoped to use them as part of my showcase at the trade show. The purchase of the stones had taken a large chunk of capital from the store's account.

"They'll do for starters. Give them to me."

No, no, *no*. This can't be happening. Not again. The stern clench of his jaw reminds me of the danger in crossing him. Slowly, I remove the earrings and unclasp the bracelet. He extends a hand, waiting for me to give them over. My fingertips brush his palm, sending tingles up my arms. My mind and body are at war over this man. Is he a protector? A lover? My enemy?

"Very nice. Did you make these, too?"

"Yes." Animosity rages in my tone. Self-entitled bastard. At the same time, I'm thrilled by his praise.

"And what do you think they're worth?" He dangles the bracelet from a fingertip. The jewels glitter seductively in the soft light of his bedroom.

"The bracelet is worth five thousand and the earrings about two."

"Great." He shoves them into his pants pocket, ignoring my protests. "What about the dress?"

"What about it?" I smooth my hands over the silky blue fabric.

"It looks great on you."

"Thanks."

"Take it off." At the drop of my jaw, he chuckles. The dirty bastard enjoys making me uncomfortable. "It must be worth four or five grand, right?"

"Maybe." The intensity of his gaze stirs more confusion into the evening. I don't want to like the way his pupils darken when he looks at my mouth. My response is crazy, yet I crave more. More praise. More danger. "I'm pretty sure it's too small for you."

His laughter booms through the room. "Oh, man, you're something else." The smile slips from his handsome face. He twirls a finger in the air. "Take it off. Don't make me ask again."

Part of me wants to challenge his authority. I weigh the consequences of rebellion. What's the worst he could do? The sinister twist of his lips suggests I don't want to know. However threatening his gaze, I'm not afraid. I lift my chin. "And what if I don't?"

"I'll take it off for you." When I don't budge, his eyes narrow. "Or I could bring your friend here. What was her name? Emeline? I'm sure Gage could keep her busy for a few hours." The thought of Em knowing about my stupidity is worse than whatever Cash has in mind. To underscore his threat, he withdraws my phone from his pocket. "What's your passcode?" I bite my lower lip. "No? That's okay. I already know it." He unlocks the phone and holds it up so that I can see the display.

"If I do this, can I go home?" I long for the safety and security of my cozy cottage.

"You can go home, but not tonight." He taps out a quick text, reading the words aloud in time with the dexterous movements of his fingers. "Hey, Em. All good. Spending the night. See you tomorrow," then hits send. He tosses the phone onto the cushion at his side. "Now, let's get to business. You and me need some time to work out the terms of our new arrangement."

"You're evil," I whisper.

"That and a whole lot worse." My insult seems to please him. "So what's it going to be, Jagger?"

"Fine." I reach over my shoulder for the zipper, but the tab hovers out of reach. "A little help would be nice."

I can tell by the twist of his lips that he's not thrilled about the idea. The heels of my shoes wobble as I walk over to him and stand between his spread knees. He places both palms on his thighs, stares up at me, then stands. I lift my hair and turn my back to him. He brushes a few stray locks from my neck. The glide of his fingers over my skin starts a chain reaction inside my body. A wave of heat. A jolt of electricity. Dampness between my thighs. The zipper growls as he drags it down the length of the dress. One fingertip traces the groove of my spine and halts at the top of my panties. The touch seems to last forever. With each inch, I can't help considering how his fingers might feel on the rest of my body, on my breasts, inside my pussy. I know it's insane, but I'm attracted to his power and confidence. The tenderness in his touch hints to a gentler side. I want to learn more about him. He fascinates me in a way no man ever has before.

When I turn to face him, his pupils overtake the color of his irises. I slip the dress from my shoulders. The filmy material lands in a puddle at my feet. His enigmatic gaze crawls down the length of my torso, over my bra and the tiny triangle of fabric covering my sex. Less than six inches separates his chest from mine. One deep breath will bring my taut nipples into contact with his solid pectorals. He retreats, shoving a hand through his hair.

"Pick it up." The gravel in his voice suggests my nakedness affects him. I bend over, giving him an eyeful of my backside, then drape the dress over the arm of the couch. In response, he unbuttons his shirt and tosses it on the nearest chair. Lord have mercy, he's a spectacle of rippling abs and ink. I bobble on my stilettos. To keep my balance, I place a hand on the nearest chair.

My voice cracks as I ask, "Are we going to have sex?" Please let the answer be yes. Maybe then I can get rid of this ache between my thighs and knock down a little of the debt at the same time. I know it's wrong to trade my body, but banging him will be more of a pleasure than a duty.

"I haven't heard you beg for it yet." Humor adds a lilt to his statement. His strong fingers go to his belt, unfasten the buckle, then lower the zip of his fly. He steps out his pants, folds them neatly, and lays them next to the shirt. Black boxer briefs hug his narrow hips and highlight an impressive erection. He's big. Big enough to make my throat close up. Finding enough oxygen to fill my lungs becomes a struggle. One corner of his mouth twitches in a lopsided smirk. "Then again, I'm just getting started."

NINE

Jagger

In the morning, I try to sneak into the house without Emeline seeing me. I go in the kitchen entrance, shoes in hand, and tiptoe down the hall toward my bedroom. Two steps from the door, my progress comes to a halt when she steps out of the bathroom, her hair wrapped in a towel, freshly showered. Her gaze sweeps over my clothing—or lack of—before meeting my eyes.

"Hey," I say, keeping my tone light and airy as I breeze past her, ducking my head to let my hair hide my face.

"Jagger." Her footsteps follow me into my room. "Where are your clothes?"

"Um, I spilled something on my dress, so Cash gave me a shirt to wear." As soon as the lie passes my lips, the guilt is overwhelming. I hate lying to her. "If you don't mind, I'm going to grab a quick shower and I'll meet you at the store."

"Yes, I mind. What happened? I was worried sick." From beneath the screen of my hair, I catch a glimpse of her expression. The reproach on her face almost brings me to tears. I can't keep up this charade for long. "A guy drops you off in his dress shirt and no panties, and you're acting like it's nothing. I need details."

"Look, I promise to tell you everything, but right now, I need a hot shower."

Her heavy sigh fills the silence. "Okay, but I'm going to hold you to that. Clean up and then I want the whole story. All of it," she adds, sternly.

"Promise." I grab my robe from the hook in my bedroom then step into the bathroom, close the door between us, and lean back against the cool wood, relieved to be alone for the first time since Cash picked me up last night.

In front of the mirror, I unbutton the shirt, pausing to draw in the scent of his cologne still clinging to the linen.

"Hey, Jag. I left my phone in there. I'm just gonna grab—"

Before I can stop her, Em opens the door. Under normal circumstances, this wouldn't be a big deal. We've lived together for a long time. This morning, however, I'm mortified. I grab a towel and try to cover myself, but not before she gets an eyeful of my naked body.

"Jesus." She sucks in a shocked breath. "What the fuck did he do to you?"

My reflection in the mirror reveals a truth I can't

hide. I shift the towel higher to hide the hickeys on my breasts. Round fingertip bruises dot my thighs and throat. It's my face that betrays me. My lips are pink and swollen. I touch them gingerly. The brush of my fingertips brings back a rush of memories. I close my eyes, squeezing them tight to fight back the titillating images flooding my head.

"Oh, Jag. Did he—did he—" She pauses to clear her throat. "Do I need to call the police?"

"No. No." I grab her arm to keep her from making the call. "It wasn't like that. He didn't—we never—I mean, it was consensual."

Her eyebrows lift. "You're one freaky bitch, Jagger Jones."

"We didn't have sex. Technically." I wave a hand through the air, like that will help my case, not sure where the line is drawn between foreplay and fucking. "It's complicated."

"Apparently." With a confused shrug, she backs out of the room. "All right. Take your shower. Meanwhile, I'll be waiting impatiently to hear this story."

"Thanks." I give her a tight smile then exhale a sigh of relief when the door closes behind her.

The cleansing spray of water does little to erase the events of the previous night. With each glide of the loofah over my skin, I feel his hands on my breasts and the scrape of his beard against my inner thighs. I squeeze my eyes shut, but the memories won't stop.

Even today, his question echoes through the hollow space between my ribs: "What's it going to be, Jagger?"

"I'll stay." Those two words had sealed my fate. What choice did I have? Sex with a hot guy seemed like the simplest answer, so I agreed. "But I won't beg you for it."

"Really? Wanna bet on it?" The cockiness in his voice spurred my competitive streak.

"Sure."

He moved closer, drawing his fingertips across his flat belly. "Name your stakes."

"If I win, you forgive the debt."

"Can't do that, little girl." He took another step, bringing us toe to toe. "Try again."

"Double or nothing," I replied.

"That's a bold wager. Especially when you ain't seen what I'm bringing to the table." His arrogance, combined with the heat in his eyes, made me a little bit insane. Why else would I make a bet over sex with a known criminal?

"You're not as attractive as you think. Not to me." My words matched his in confidence. However, he knows I'm lying. I want him more than I've ever wanted any man.

"I beg to differ." He leaned down, placing his nose next to my ear, scenting my hair like an alpha male about to choose his female. I raised my chin. No matter what happened, I wasn't going to let him see how he affected me. He toyed with a lock of my hair between his thumb and forefinger before moving around me in a slow circle. "You've been giving me the eye since I walked into your store. You want it. I know you want it.

Let's make this easy. Just admit it, and we can move on."

When he was behind me, he paused to press his lips to the nape of my neck. I shivered, unable to control my response to his hot mouth on my bare skin. He continued to brush light kisses along my shoulder, my collarbone, the ticklish spot behind my ear. I gulped, the sound audible. "You're an arrogant bastard."

"Aw, but you like that about me, don't you?" He exhaled. His breath heated my earlobe. "Give yourself a break, Jagger. I promise you'll enjoy it." The edges of his teeth nibbled along the shell of my ear, and it was like a direct hotline to my pussy. "And no bets. This isn't about business this is pleasure—for both of us. I want you to beg for it because you want me inside you. Balls deep. Banging that pussy until you come."

The filthy talk kindled a fire between my legs. He came to a stop in front of me, rested his forehead against mine, and kissed the corner of my mouth. My inner muscles clenched. If only he'd touch me down there. "Do you kiss your mamma with that dirty mouth?"

"You ain't seen nothing yet." With one hand, he grabbed my bottom, his fingers digging into the cleft of my ass, and yanked my hips to his. I gasped at the hard steel rod pressed against my stomach. His opposite hand snaked to the back of my head, and then he *took* my mouth. Claimed it in a kiss so deep and so wet that my knees almost buckled. His tongue dueled with mine, searching every inch of real estate, until I grew dizzy from lack of oxygen and the flood of endorphins. He stripped away the barrier that encased my darkest desires and turned them loose. I dug my fingers into his hair and grinded against him, wild with need.

When he finally released me, I panted, desperate to catch my breath. We stood staring at each other, his cock tenting the front of his shorts and my nipples pointing through the satin bra cups. It had only been a kiss, but it had been as intimate as fucking. I dragged the back of my forearm over my wet mouth. "Is that all you've got?" I asked with more sass than brains.

"Oh, darlin'," he drawled. "I haven't even started yet."

The water from the shower is starting to cool. I have no idea how long I've been standing under the stream. All I know is that the memories of last night are enough to bring me to the brink of orgasm. I slip two fingers between my legs, eager to relieve the ache before I implode.

"Do you like it when I fuck your mouth?" His dirty whisper echoed in my ears.

Unable to speak, I nodded. He clenched his fingers in my hair, holding my head in place while his cock slipped through my lips. The crown touched the back of my throat. Tears ran down my cheeks. I tried to rub my clit, eager to relieve the ache, but he grabbed my hands and pinned them behind my back.

"Not yet. Not unless you beg for it." He dragged his dick out of my mouth. The red tip bobbed in front of my nose. "Do you want me to fuck you now, Jagger? All you have to do is say please."

I take my time getting dressed. My body aches from exhaustion and the strain of overworked muscles. On the drive to the store, I almost run a stop sign thinking about the way things had ended with Cash this morning.

"Spread your legs. Let me taste that pussy." His nasty words echoed in my ears. His hand slipped between my thighs and rubbed the tight nub. I followed his command, blinded by my lust.

I grabbed his cock and tugged him toward me. The thick, protruding veins formed ridges on his shaft. Ridges that would have felt like ecstasy inside me. My walls pulsed, ready for orgasm.

"Hands over your head. Grab the headboard." His voice was low and raspy, scratching all the dark and dirty places inside my head.

My fingers wrapped around the rungs of the painted wood. The tip of his nose slid along my seam. I jerked my hips upward, eager for whatever came next. His tongue dragged through the tender folds between my legs. My knuckles ached from my tight hold on the headboard. One of his fingers penetrated the tight ring of muscle in my bottom and curled upward. I jerked at the surprise intrusion. His chuckle vibrated against my thigh. A second finger entered my pussy, followed by a third.

He filled me, all of me. I came in a torrent of cries and tears and pleas to make it stop and to never stop. To my credit, I never begged for him to fuck me. But I was so close to surrendering. With one hand buried inside me, he lurched to his knees. He came on my stomach in hot spurts and a frenzy of groans.

The intensity of my orgasm lasted an eternity. When he'd finished, he grabbed a washcloth from the bathroom and cleaned me up. I unclenched my fingers from the headboard, certain I'd never be the same again. Once I was clean, Cash dotted kisses along my over-heated skin. He rested his chin on my sternum and grinned up at me. I ran my fingers through his glossy hair, loving the softness between my fingers.

Sin and mischief glimmered in his eyes. "So much for round one. Are you ready to go again?"

A knock on my car window jerks me from the memory. I have no idea how long I've been sitting in the store parking lot. A minute? Ten? The UPS guy smiles and motions for me to roll down my window. My cheeks flame with embarrassment as he passes an overnight envelope into the car.

"Can you sign for this?" he asks. "I'm running behind."

"Sure." I scrawl my name with a shaking hand and muster a smile. He probably thinks I'm insane. Maybe I am. I had four orgasms with Cash, and I'm ready for more. I don't care that he's a criminal. In fact, his lawless spirit turns me on.

When I walk into the store, Em is so involved in inventory that she doesn't notice my entrance. I toss my purse into the desk drawer, lay the envelope on the counter, and head for the gallery.

"Oh, no you don't." Her reproach catches me with my hand on the doorknob. *So close.* I turn and give her a weary smile. The playful light is missing from her eyes. "Do you have the bracelets and earrings you wore last night? I want to get them back inside the display."

My heart sinks. After the trauma of Hubert Spillman's death, the encounter with Kyle, and the bet with Cash, the loss of the jewelry had seemed insignificant. Not so much now. I can't look at her. I'm in so deep. Up to my eyeballs. I shift from one foot to the other, training my attention on the pressed tin ceiling of the office. "Yes and no."

Hearing the note of dismay in my voice, she drops her pencil onto the desk and comes around to sit on the front of it. "What does that mean?"

"I fucked up, Em. Big time. And I have no idea how to get out of it."

"Okay." Seeing the tears in my eyes, she rubs my shoulder, her expression tender. "It can't be that bad. Tell me what's going on and we'll fix it."

"You can't fix this. No one can." I wrap my arms around my waist, wishing I could evaporate into thin air.

"Bullshit. I'm a fantastic fixer. And you know how I love a challenge." Under different circumstances, I'd find her determination endearing.

"It's so complicated. I don't know where to begin."

She smiles and settles back onto the desk, letting her legs swing. "That's easy. Start at the beginning."

TEN

Jagger

My life is filled with so many lies, I'm not sure where the truth begins and the deceptions end. Emeline's sympathetic expression buoys my confidence. Unable to sit, I pace the wood floor in front of the shelves and wring my hands while I decide how much she needs to know. "About a year ago, I stole a necklace from a jewelry store. It was easy. I made a copy, walked into the showroom, and replaced the original with my fake when the salesperson wasn't looking." Em's mouth gapes open. I lift a hand. "I know. I know. It was wrong and stupid and I feel terrible about it."

"Why would you do something like that?"

"I guess I wanted to prove to myself that my work was good enough to pass." Spoken aloud, the excuse sounds hollow. "That was the first time."

"There was more than one time?" With a shocked

gasp, she shoves back into the chair, making the castors squeak.

"Jimmy sold the pieces to an underground dealer, and I gave him twenty percent for keeping his mouth shut. The last store I stole from belonged to Cash. Anyway, Cash started asking around and he ended up here." She starts to speak, but I interrupt. "Hang on. It gets worse."

"How can it possibly get any worse?" I can tell how uncomfortable my confession is making her by the way she crosses her arms over her chest. "Okay. Keep going."

"So, he came in here and demanded payment, and when I couldn't pay him, he took the Stella Valentine photograph. And then I couldn't pay for the photo, so I got a payday loan and slipped it into the account when you weren't looking." Embarrassment burns my face.

"Why didn't you tell me? We could've worked out an installment plan or something."

"There's more."

"More?" Her eyebrows lift incredulously.

"It seems my sister owes him money—a lot of money—and now he wants me to pay her debt, too."

"When you say a lot, what exactly does that mean?"

"Two hundred thousand?"

Em purses her lips, the way she does when she's thinking hard. "When your grandma died, she didn't really leave you any money, did she?" It's not a question. "That was Callie's money."

"Yes." I've been holding in the truth for so long that

the words tumble out in a rush. "When she escaped from Cash, she gave me the money to start over in a new life. I bought twenty percent of Mr. Mercer's business, our house, and this building we work in. I thought they were sound investments. I've spent all of it, Em—every last penny—trying to keep the business afloat. And last night, Cash said he had a job for me, a way to pay him back, but I botched it up. So he took the bracelet and earrings and my dress as part of the repayment, and now I owe him an extra fifty thousand dollars."

Em closes her eyes and grips her skull with both hands like she has a headache. I can't blame her because my head hurts, too. "Shit, Jagger. This is bad. Really, *really* bad."

"I know." I continue pacing.

"First of all, I'm hurt that you lied to me." The reproach in her expression cuts through my chest like a dagger.

"I wanted to tell you, but I was embarrassed, and he kept threatening to hurt you. I didn't want to drag you into my mess."

"Who took you to the hospital when Kyle pushed you down the stairs? And who hid you from him until the cops could pick him up?"

"You did." I lick the dryness from my lips. "I forgot to mention that Kyle was at Cash's club. He cornered me in the bathroom, but Cash came in and saved me."

"Wait? He's out of prison?" The color fades from her face.

"He said he got an early release. But I have a

restraining order. Now that he knows I'm with Cash, he won't bother me." At least, I hope he won't.

"This is crazy, Jag. How did it get to this?"

She's right. Nothing I say will excuse my bad behavior. Of all the people in my life, she's the one who matters most. "I'm so, so sorry, Em."

Her heavy sigh ruffles the loose wisps of hair around her face. "Just so we're clear, you're not forgiven, but you can make it up to me later. Right now, we need to figure out how to get Cash out of your life." She taps her pink polished fingernails on the desk. "Isn't there a way to reach your sister? Maybe she can help."

"No. No way. I don't want to involve her. She went to a lot of trouble to escape Cash. The last thing I want to do is subject her to him again."

"I have so many questions, I don't even know where to start." Shaking her head, she grabs her phone. "I'm calling Tony. Maybe he can help."

I snatch the phone away from her before she can initiate the call. "No. No way. You can't tell anyone, especially not Tony."

"Cash must be breaking a zillion laws. Tony will know how to handle it."

"Guys like Cash are above the law. If you tell Tony, it will only put him in harm's way. You don't want that, do you?" Some twisted part of me feels loyal to Cash. I'm no longer afraid of him. Although he's been a menace, I don't wish him any harm.

Her somber eyes study me. After a long minute, she nods. "Fine. I won't say anything. Not yet."

"I shouldn't have dragged you into this, but I'm so glad to have you on my side. You have to promise not to tell a soul. No one."

"All right. I promise." To signify her sincerity, she draws a cross over her heart. "But there's one more thing I don't understand."

I nod. "What's that?"

"If he's done all these terrible things, why did you sleep with him?" When I open my mouth to dispute the term, she shakes her head. "Or whatever it is that you did? What is this hold he has over you?"

"I don't know." But I do. The minute his lips touched mine, I was lost to him. "He so confident. Invincible. I've never met anyone like him. He's tough but tender. When he touches me—" I shiver. "The sex—it was unbelievable. Mind blowing." The next part is more difficult to admit. "I'd do it again if he asked."

What I can't tell Em is about this morning. The way he held me in his arms after giving me one orgasm after another. We watched the sun rise over the lake and listened to the water lapping on the shore through the open balcony doors. It had felt right. Perfect.

"That girl—Chelle—was she your girlfriend?" That kind of question threatened to ruin the mood, but I had to ask him.

"I should get you home." He started to unwrap his arms from around my waist. I tightened my embrace, wanting this peaceful interlude to continue for a few more minutes. Once we left his bed, we'd become enemies again, and I wasn't ready. Not yet.

"Wait. Just a few more minutes. I'm so comfortable." I snuggled deeper into the warmth of his chest. He smelled like me, like sex. "I didn't mean to upset you. It's just—I don't know anything about you."

His chin rested on top of my head. "I don't like to live in the past. Today and tomorrow are all that matters."

"I get it." I trailed my fingers along the length of his arm. "Can you at least tell my why Reaper is so angry with you?"

A few minutes pass before he answers. "I left the Disciples of Rage because I had bigger plans for my life. I didn't want to be a slave to their bullshit. Reaper is powerful, but he's just a petty criminal. Boosting cars, dealing drugs, prostitution—those things only lead in one direction—prison. Diamonds are where it's at." He tapped my forearm with an index finger, drew back to look me in the eyes. "I saw a way out, and I took it. Gage came with me. We had no idea that the price of freedom would be so high."

"What was—?" My question was cut off when he rolled me underneath him.

"No more questions." His lips found the tender skin beneath my ear and sucked until I squirmed. My gasp seemed to satisfy him. He hopped out of bed, strutting naked across the floor, giving me a glorious view of his taut ass and tossed his dress shirt at me. "Time to get up, lazy bones. I've got a big day ahead of me."

I t's Sunday and the store is closed, thank goodness. Em and I sit on the couch in our living room and brainstorm ways to repay Cash. A *Lifetime* movie plays on the TV but neither of us is watching. Rain patters against the windowpanes. I draw a knit throw over my bare feet to drive away the chill, but I know the weather is only partly responsible for the icy dread in the pit of my stomach.

Em moves to the armchair and curls up with one foot tucked beneath her. A pair of glasses is perched on her nose. She taps her notepad with the eraser of her pencil. "This is hopeless. There's no way you can repay that much money without some kind of divine intervention."

"I know. Mr. Mercer will be back at the store soon. He'll want to go over the inventory and the accounts." When he finds out, he's going to be so disappointed in me. I clutch my head in a desperate attempt to gather my composure. "What am I going to do?"

"I can't lie to him, Jag." Em's oval-shaped face tightens.

"You won't have to." My resolve to protect my two favorite people grows. Em and Mr. Mercer both have such good hearts. Neither deserves this.

"He might press charges. You could go to jail." The realization brings tears to her eyes.

"No one is going to jail." My words carry false confidence. My little Chihuahua, Lucy, leaps into my lap, sensing my distress, and bumps my hand with her paw, demanding attention. When I don't respond quickly enough, she flops onto her back and kicks her legs. I rub her soft puppy belly, taking comfort in her unconditional joy. The thought of jail always seemed like a distant improbability, but now I can see how foolish I've been.

"You could take out a mortgage on the building." Emeline's voice lilts hopefully.

"It's only worth about a hundred thousand, and my credit's not so good anymore." The store hasn't turned a profit in the last year. Most of my disposable income has been spent on a new roof, furnace repairs, and leaky plumbing.

The doorbell interrupts our conversation. When I open the door, a florist and her assistant bring in four dozen blood red roses. "We don't usually do Sunday deliveries, but your boyfriend was very insistent. You must be one lucky lady." She winks at me.

"He's not my boyfriend," I reply and close the door behind her. They line the flowers along the length of the breakfast bar, offer a clipboard for my signature then leave.

Together, Emeline and I stare at the gorgeous crystal vases. She shakes her head. "I'm confused." The heady scent of fresh flowers fills the room. "He extorts and blackmails you then sends you roses. Is he trying to kill you or date you?"

"Date me? That's ridiculous." To emphasize my feelings on the subject, I roll my eyes. Despite my denial, I have to admit his actions muddy the waters of our already complicated relationship.

With a heavy heart, I take out a high interest mortgage on my house and the store building and come up with about half the money owed to Cash. I know it's not enough, but it's the best I can do under the circumstances. All I can do is hope that we gain enough new business through the upcoming trade show to raise store profits and cover the installment payments.

To make matters worse, Mr. Mercer's health isn't improving. After a series of small strokes, he moves to a nursing home where he can get continuous care. I take time away from work to make sure he's settled. Most of the time he's sharp and loveable, but when I visit later in the week, he calls me Hattie.

"He's been like this all day," the nurse says in the hallway when I leave his room. "Don't take it personally."

"I won't." Although I manage a rueful smile, emotion burns my eyes. He's been my rock for the past two years. If I lose him, his absence will leave a hole in my heart that might never heal.

I'm swiping my eyes on the way to my Honda when I hear a familiar masculine voice. "Hey, girl."

My pulse stutters. Cash leans against the front fender of my car with his hands in the pockets of his jeans. A tight black turtleneck hugs every dip and swell of his muscular chest. I slow my steps, seeking time to gather my thoughts. Why now? It seems like I can never catch a break.

"How's your friend?" he asks, his tone casual. I could almost—*almost*—believe that he cares.

"Not so good." Despite my best efforts, my voice breaks. I dig through my purse for my keys, hindered by the blur of tears.

"Hey, hey. Slow down. Look at me." When I don't react, he takes my purse, sets it on the hood of the car, then tilts my chin up to him. His brown eyes are reassuring. "What's wrong? Tell me."

I glance to the garden beyond the parking lot, wanting to hide my emotions from him. "Why should I confide in you? You never tell me anything." Anger boils beneath the surface of my calm expression. Life is so unfair. I need to lash out at someone—anyone—to release the pressure of always being strong.

"I tell you what you need to know."

"Wrong answer." I try to step around him, but he blocks my path with his broad shoulders.

"I'm reaching out here, Jag. Trying to open up a dialogue about more than gems and money. You say you want to know me. Well, I need to know you, too." The naked honesty in his voice brings my startled gaze to his. "I'm trying to do better. I wouldn't ask if I didn't care."

"If you care so much, why are you putting me through this hell?" I give his chest a shove, ignoring the startled glance of an employee heading into the building.

"Because I see potential in you, baby girl." His fingers wrap around my wrist. "Without pressure, a diamond is nothing more than a lump of coal."

His declaration soothes the raging inferno inside my chest. No one ever thought I would amount to anything. Not my parents, nor my grandma, nor my teachers. Even Callie. She always looked upon me as a burden, someone to be sheltered and protected. As if I wasn't capable of making my own decisions in life.

"I'm so worried about him. He's the only person who believes in me."

"I believe in you, too, Jagger. Or I wouldn't be here." With a sweep of his little finger, he brushes the hair away from my face. "Talk to me. Maybe I can help.

He settles back against the fender, arms crossed over his chest, and listens while I tell him the whole story of Mr. Mercer, his kindnesses, and his mentorship. Cash doesn't react, but he listens—*really* listens—to every single word. When I'm done, his strong arms wrap around me in a hug. I hold onto him, my face buried in his shoulder, breathing in his clean scent. For a brief moment, I feel safe and protected. His lips brush the top of my head. "Sounds like he needs you as much as you need him. You're gonna need to be strong for him."

"I know." After a minute, I disentangle from his embrace. No matter how good his arms feel, I can't allow myself to misinterpret his pity for affection. I clear my throat. "I'm fine now. Thanks."

"All right." He returns his hands to his pockets. I back up to reclaim my personal space. His mouth twitches like he's amused by my desperate attempt to stay in control. "Let's talk business then. You got my money yet?"

"Seriously?"

He shrugs.

"I don't have it with me." I snatch my purse from the hood and resume the search for my keys. "It's at my house."

"Great." Two delicious dimples bracket his mouth. "Let's go get it."

ELEVEN

Cash

I've been dying to get an inside glimpse of Jagger's crib since we met, and it doesn't disappoint. The kitchen smells like chocolate chip cookies, evoking childhood memories of my grandmother's kitchen. My family had been happy back then. Before Dad became obsessed with money and power and keeping secrets. Appliances clutter the counter, but the surfaces sparkle. A round rag rug covers the worn hardwood floor. I drink up every square inch of the space for clues about her likes and dislikes. Lots of books suggest a love of reading. A dog bed in the corner for the yapping ball of fur at our feet. Everything here has meaning for her. I could spend hours analyzing her choices.

She tosses her purse on the breakfast bar, pats the dog then goes to the cabinet above the fridge, and pulls down two cereal boxes. She places them on the counter and slides them toward me. "Here. It's all there. You can count it."

I peek inside. Stacks of hundreds are wrapped in rubber bands. "I trust you." I draw out fifty thousand and slide it back to her.

"What's this?" Her forehead furrows.

"For you."

"I don't understand." She stares at the money.

"You need the money, right? There you go. Consider it a bonus for your hard work."

Anger flashes across her sculpted features. "You extorted me, and you're giving the money back?"

"I asked you to repay a debt, and you did. Take the cash, Jagger. It was more about honor and principle than money."

"I had to apply for mortgages to get that money. You have no idea what I went through." Her shout echoes off the tile backsplash.

"On a building and house that you bought with cash stolen from me."

I face her, toe-to-toe, our noses an inch from touching. We glare at each other. I love the way her nostrils quiver when she's angry. The lines of her body come alive. One of these days, I'm going to fuck all that anger out of her, and it's going to be everything.

After a few seconds, her shoulders lower. "Okay. Fair point." She drags the money toward her and scoops it into one of the drawers. "Do you want something to drink?"

"Sure. What you got?" While she runs through a list

of beverages, I peek into the adjoining living room. Pink and white pillows cover the blue sofa. Her TV is small, nothing like my enormous flat screen, and the furnishings are worn but comfortable.

"Cash?" She calls to me from the open refrigerator.

"I'll have a bottled water. Thanks." I walk over to where she's standing. There's a picture of her and Emeline on the refrigerator. I pull the photo free from the magnet holding it in place. "Where was this taken?"

"Um, Philadelphia." Her nose wrinkles adorably as she glances at the picture. "We lived there for a while. That's the Liberty Bell behind us."

"Right." I return the picture to the refrigerator and take the water bottle from her extended hand. "You like to travel?"

"Sure. Don't you?" She leans against the counter, tucking a loose strand of hair behind her ear.

"Love it." Seeing her here, in her home space, makes her even more attractive. I'm dying to know what makes her tick, how to please her. "If you could go anywhere in the world, where would it be?"

"Santorini. Athens. Crete."

"Greece? You like old shit like the Parthenon and the Acropolis?" I take a drink from the bottle then set it on the counter and inch toward her. I can't be near her without wanting to touch her.

"Yes." Her dark eyes sparkle with enthusiasm. "Don't you?"

"Sometimes." I take her water bottle from her hand and set it next to mine. "Why don't you go?"

Her lips part as I approach. The swell of her breasts rises and falls. "Because I owe some dick a lot of money and can't afford it."

Laughter bursts from my throat. This girl—she's so full of fire and sass—and I love that about her. I draw my fingertips down the side of her face. "Maybe I can help you out."

"Right." She scoffs and tries to look away, but I take her chin in my hand, forcing her to look at me.

"No, I'm serious." For reasons I don't want to explore, I feel guilty for the hell I've rained upon her. "Tell me what you want."

"I want to wake up feeling safe. I'm tired of looking over my shoulder, wondering who's behind me." Tears glimmer in her eyes, but she's too proud to let them fall.

"Is someone bothering you, baby girl?" A surge of protective rage sweeps through me. The thought of anyone harming her unleashes the beast inside me. If she was mine, I'd make sure no one ever touched her but me. I'd make love to her every night, buy her nice things, and show her the world.

"You mean, besides you?" The corner of her mouth twitches with a suppressed smile.

"Have I ever hurt you?" I've never raised a hand to a woman. Not once. And I never will. A fact she doesn't need to know. Fear can be a powerful motivator.

"No but you make threats." The stubborn jut of her chin brushes my palm.

"We talked about this." I sweep my thumb over her lower lip, thinking about how sweet her kiss will taste.

"I use pressure to get what I want. Pressure makes diamonds. *You* are a diamond."

The temptation overpowers my self-control. I lower my mouth to hers. Her lips are velvety soft. One of her hands curls around the back of my neck. This kiss is tender, slow, and savoring with only a hint of tongue. I close my eyes to concentrate on the sensations. It would be so easy to lose myself in her, but that's a luxury I can't afford. I pull away before I forget who I am. As I like to remind her, I'm the bad guy, and bad guys never get the girl.

"I need to go." I push away from her and rub the back of my neck to erase the lingering touch of her fingers.

I leave her standing in the kitchen and exit through the back door. On my way to my Range Rover, I notice a rusty green pickup truck parked across the street. I've seen that truck before, but I can't quite place it. The driver slouches down in the seat when I stare too long, revs the engine, and drives away. He's gone before I can catch up to him, but I manage to catch a glimpse of the guy's face. It's the jerk who cornered Jagger at my club.

TWELVE

Jagger

On the day of the Las Vegas showcase, I'm forced to push thoughts of Cash aside. Today has to go well. Sales at the store have fallen to an all-time low. Mr. Mercer isn't able to attend. Although his health is stable, he isn't strong enough for the trip. Emeline stays behind to run the store. I'm on my own, and the pressure is killing me.

Bright lights and glitter illuminate the hotel ballroom. My small booth is overpowered by the sleek, sumptuous displays of our competitors. The men wear tuxedos. The women wear expensive gowns. I borrowed Em's red off-the-shoulder dress for the event. It's a little tight around the hips but flatters my waistline and dark hair. At least I have that going for me.

Because our booth is located in the distant corner of the room, only a few buyers give us a second glance. By the end of the day, my high expectations have been flattened. We haven't made a single sale.

"Nothing?" Em asks when I call her to commiserate. "Are our prices too high?"

"From what I can tell, they're on point." I rub the exhaustion from my eyes, no longer concerned about smudging my mascara. "Maybe my designs aren't as good as we thought."

"Don't even go there." Her unwavering confidence in my skills warms my heart. "Tomorrow will be better."

"Let's hope so." I wave goodbye to Ruth and Dean in the lobby. They're going out for dinner and drinks. Even though they've invited me along, I need time alone to lick my wounds and recharge before tomorrow. I decide to get room service and turn in early.

"Have a drink and take a long soak in that gorgeous hotel bathtub." The soothing tone of Em's voice eases my panic. "Call me tomorrow."

"I will. Have a great night." I step onto the elevator, my head down as I search for my hotel key card in the depths of my purse. It seems like half my life is spent digging around my purse for keys.

A man and woman follow me into the car, boarding just as the doors start to close. I have a quick glimpse of a woman's feet in sky-high Louboutins, shiny black men's shoes and the crisp pleat of black trousers. His arm reaches across my line of sight to press the button for the floor below me. My stomach drops at the black tattoo on the back of his hand.

It's him. Cash. And he looks better than any man has a right to in a black suit, black shirt, and tie. Diamond cufflinks sparkle at his wrists. Probably a carat each. Cushion cut. Exquisite.

"Having a good time?" His deep voice rattles the tattered shreds of my composure. He's different tonight. His words are measured and sophisticated, devoid of their usual casual slang. Another facet to his already complicated persona.

I lean back against the wall for support, too tired to care about things like civility. "What are you doing here?"

The woman at his side is about my age, tall and blonde. She curls her fingers around the crook of his elbow. Her ears and neck are dripping in ice. His hand rests on the small of her back. They make a stunning couple. A wave of jealousy catches me by surprise. Of course he has women in his life. He's too yummy to be celibate. For a heartbeat, I wish I were on his arm, heading back to his hotel room for a night of headboard banging sex. The thought of him on top of this gorgeous girl stirs up feelings I don't want to acknowledge.

"Just checking up on some investments." His dark eyes travel the length of my red dress before returning to my face. An electric tingle travels to the space between my legs at the heat in his gaze. "Did you sell anything?"

"Not as much as I had hoped." I hesitate to divulge details, afraid he'll demand another payment if he thinks we did well. Yet, I don't want him to know how devastated I feel about the poor sales.

"Well, I'm sure tomorrow will be even better. Have

a nice evening, Ms. Jones." The elevator arrives at the eleventh floor. He ushers his date into the hallway. I watch them until the doors close.

His appearance dampens my already sour mood. What is he doing here? And who is that woman? Are they serious or did he pick her up for a one-night stand? The questions roll around in my head, repeating on a loop.

After an hour in my hotel room, I can't stand knowing Cash is with that woman while I'm alone, wondering if he's inside her. In need of a distraction, I decide to visit the hotel club. I touch up my makeup, smooth my hair, and head downstairs for a nightcap.

The club is packed with patrons of the jewelry show. I manage to find a single barstool on the backside of the dance floor and order a mojito. The young man at my right spins his barstool to face me. He's about my age, medium height and build, with pleasant features. A nice, normal guy. The kind I never go for.

"You look lonely." His smile is warm and friendly. "I'm here on my own, too. Can I keep you company?"

"Um, sure. I guess." Over his shoulder, a familiar dark head catches my attention. Cash is seated in the VIP section with several other men in suits. His blonde companion is nowhere to be seen. He smooths a hand over his tie, scanning the room. Our eyes meet. My heart skips a beat. The music grows louder.

"What's your name?" The guy leans closer, blocking my view of Cash.

"Jagger." I shift to keep Cash in my line of sight. He

continues to stare at me. One of his eyebrows lifts. Even from a distance, I can sense his amusement in seeing me here.

"I'm Will Warren, but everyone calls me Warren. Nice to meet you." He shakes my hand. His fingers wrap around mine a little too long. I wriggle from his grasp and drop my hand into my lap.

Bodies bob and sway on the dance floor. I catch glimpses of Cash through the haze of fog and laser lights. Several women have joined his group. A brunette balances on the arm of his chair. Each time she trails her fingers over his shoulder, my ribcage constricts.

"So where are you from?" Warren yells.

"Indiana," I shout at the same time the music stops. My declaration shatters the air. Warren bursts out laughing. A blush heats my face.

"I've never been to Indiana." When he smiles, he's more attractive. He brushes a hand over his short hair. His gaze follows mine to Cash. "You keep looking over there. Do you know that guy?"

"Oh, no. No, no." I laugh and shake my head. "It's just—those people must be pretty important. I've always wondered what it would be like to sit behind the velvet ropes."

"Me, too." He glances over his shoulder at the privileged group before giving a resigned shrug. "The blond guy in the blue suit and all the rings on his fingers— that's Braden Seaforth. He owns half the hotels on this street. The women are probably hookers. And the guy with the tattoos—that's Cash Delacorte." Hearing his name causes butterflies in my tummy. I take a sip of my drink to hide my reaction. If Warren notices, he doesn't show it. His smile slips away, and his expression sobers. "My cousin's a cop. He said if you want to make somebody disappear, Delacorte is your man. He's bad news."

"I'm sorry. I've got to go." The air is too hot. I can't breathe. I down the mojito in one long gulp then push my way through the crowd to the nearest exit, leaving Warren alone at the bar. On my left is a series of small balconies overlooking the courtyard. I burst through the first set of doors and into the cool quiet.

The edges of the balcony are screened by tall potted palms and ferns. Blossoms of bougainvillea trail over the railings. I gulp in the fresh air until my pulse settles. The past few months have been overwhelming. No wonder my nerves are frazzled. I just need a minute to pull myself together.

"Everything all right?" Cash's voice buzzes next to my ear.

I don't turn around. If I look at him, he'll see my weakness and use it against me. "I'm fine. Go back to your party."

"That's not a party. It's work." He inches closer until the heat of his body warms my backside. "Who was your friend?"

"No one." I throw the question back at him. "You seem to have lots of friends."

"Business associates." The tips of his fingers graze my collarbone as he sweeps my hair to one side.

"Who was the woman on the elevator? Are you

fucking her?" I hate myself for wanting to know more about him, but I can't help it. I shrink from his touch. He follows me, inching closer.

"Are you jealous, Jagger?" His breath puffs against my bare skin. I arch toward him, drawn by an undeniable force. The softness of his lips brushes my neck.

"Yes." There's no point in denying it. The thought of him between any woman's legs but mine turns my vision red.

"Finally we're getting somewhere." He draws my left sleeve lower and kisses my shoulder. I turn my head so I can see his expression. His pupils are large, black, infinite pools of ink.

I dig my fingers into the hard muscles of his thighs, gathering the fabric of his trousers in my grip, tugging him closer. "I need to know."

"I thought about it, but why would I settle for her when you're the one I want?" It takes a few seconds for the meaning behind his words to settle over me. A ripple of gooseflesh crosses my nape in the wake of his kisses. He nips at my earlobe. "You should know that I'm not the kind of guy to fuck around. When I'm with someone, I'm completely faithful."

My head swims with the prettiness of his words. "But we're not together, are we?"

The rough skin of his palms smooths up my arms. "Not yet."

"Are you here to collect payment? Because I don't think I can do that again." Although our encounter had been hot, the blow to my self-esteem was a price I'm no longer willing to pay. I care too much, and caring leads to heartbreak.

"I'm here because you're so damn sexy in this dress, and I was worried about you." His hands shift to cup my breasts. I grind my ass into his pelvis, pleased to feel the steel rod inside his trousers. A sharp intake of breath hisses through his teeth. "Ah, Jagger. What are you doing to me? Why can't I get you out of my head?"

I don't answer. Instead, I lift the hem of my dress to reveal my panties. His answer shifts the power in my favor. I need to feel him inside me. Just once. One time will be enough to end this ridiculous schoolgirl crush I've been carrying for him, and I can get on with my life.

No one can see us through the screen of foliage. His hand slips inside the front of my panties. One of his fingers finds my clit and drags through the wetness. The pressure between my legs continues to build, demanding release. My head falls against his chest. His kisses rain over my temple, my jaw, my neck. I moan when his fingers leave to fumble at his fly. The growl of his zipper mingles with the sounds of our harsh breathing. While he puts on a condom, I push my panties down my hips, let them fall to the floor, and step out of them. Everything about this is so wrong, but it feels so right.

"Spread your legs. Arch your back." He whispers the commands in my ear as he drags the head of his cock through the cleft of my bottom. One slow shove seats him inside me—all the way to the root. I gasp at the intrusion, the excruciating pleasure of being stretched beyond reason. It's everything I dreamed of and more. He grunts and pulls out. Repeats the movement. Once. Twice. A dozen more times. Each consecutive thrust is deeper than the previous one. It's fast, sloppy, and wild, a dark and dirty fantasy coming to life.

Voices float up from the courtyard. Cash places a hand over my mouth to quiet my moans, but he doesn't slow down. Each thrust of his hips meets my ass with a muffled thump. I'm beyond debating the wisdom of this encounter. Every choice in my life has brought me to this moment. To him.

"So freaking good," he gasps in my ear.

My orgasm rolls over me with unrivaled intensity. Shockwaves travel from my pussy to my toes and back up again. Cash's hands squeeze my breasts. His harsh breathing echoes in my ears. I want it to go on forever, because once we're done here, I'm going to war.

Too soon he's withdrawing, dealing with the condom, zipping up his pants. I tug my dress over my hips and try to calm my racing heartrate.

He slips an arm around my waist, pulling me against his chest, my back to his front. "You were right. That pussy is something special," he whispers, lips grazing my ear. "I have to go, but I'll come to your room when my meeting is over."

"No." I can hardly believe my refusal. He just rocked my world with the best sex ever. I want more, but I need to maintain some kind of control over my situation.

"No?" He chuckles. "Are you sure?"

"You're the enemy. I can't fuck you then fight you."

"Why not?" He gently turns me around to face him. A mixture of humor and tenderness bows his lips, something I've never seen before. "Fighting you is half the fun."

"I'm serious. This—" I draw a circle in the air between us. "This can't happen again."

Darkness passes over his face. "You forget who you're dealing with. You don't call the shots in this relationship. I do."

"We don't have a relationship, remember? This is business." With the edge of my finger, I wipe the outline of my lips to clean up any smudges of lipstick. I give a final tug to the hem of my dress and brush past him. "I've had a very long day. If you'll excuse me." Before I reach the door, he grabs my bicep and yanks me back to him. He's strong and male. Despite having been inside me moments earlier, I want him again.

"Wanna know why you didn't have any sales today? Because no one moves anything in this industry without my say so. I hold all the power in this game, sweet thing." His language slips back into his familiar slang. "The sooner you accept it, the better this is gonna go for you." He gives me a little shake. "Go home, little girl. You ain't ready to play with the big dogs." In the dim light, he's more sinister than ever. "I'll be out of town for a bit. You've got thirty days to make your next payment. In full. No more games."

THIRTEEN

Jagger

When I return Baxter's Corner, I relate the details of the trade show to Emeline over breakfast. Her eyes grow round as she slathers cream cheese on a bagel. "He's jealous."

"What? No way." I wave a dismissive hand through the air. "He's just being a dick."

"I think it's more than that, Jag."

"All I know is that I'm done with his head games. I'll do whatever it takes to be rid of him."

"Well, actually, I've been thinking about that, and I have an idea." Inspiration gleams in her eyes. "You know my friend, Loretta?"

I nod. "The one with the cleaning company."

"Yes. That's her." She gets out of her chair and begins to pace, bagel in one hand, gesturing with the other. "She's big time. Here in Indy, her customers live in those gorgeous million-dollar mansions around Carmel and Geist Reservoir." *People like Cash.* "Not only that, she's got satellite offices in Beverly Hills, Manhattan, Vegas, and a dozen more cities." Enthusiasm gives her fair skin a pink glow. "Rich people, Jag. Basketball players, politicians, CEOs. The thing is, she's successful but up to her eyeballs in debt. No liquid assets, and she needs cash."

I shove away the plate with my bagel, too anxious to eat. "I'm not sure what that has to do with me."

"She cleans houses, Jag. She has security codes and keys. Full access." Her face flushes with excitement. "What if she gave you pictures of their jewelry? You could make up fakes. She could switch them. We sell the real stuff. You give the money to Cash." She throws her hands up in the air. "It's a win-win situation."

"I don't know." As crazy as it sounds, her idea has merit. "Do you trust this woman?"

"Absolutely." She cocks a hip and crosses her arms over her chest. "Admit it. It's an awesome plan."

"What if we get caught?"

"You weren't worried about getting caught before."

"Of course I was. Not so much the first time, but after that—absolutely." Despite my misgivings, I have to admit the idea excites me. A theft ring run by yours truly. Talk about levelling up. With the proper planning, we could be as rich as Cash. Maybe richer.

L oretta comes to the house the next evening to discuss logistics. She's a pretty, thirty-something blonde with downturned blue eyes and a slight limp. We gather around the kitchen table to look over client lists and schedules. Emeline makes Moscow mules and serves them in the copper mugs I gave her on our first Christmas together.

"Yeah, it should be easy," she confirms while tucking a curl behind her ear. "Most of these people aren't good about locking away their jewelry. You wouldn't believe how careless they are. It's just a matter of opportunity."

"You're taking a huge risk. You understand that, right?" I want to be sure there aren't any misgivings on her part. "Once we start this, we're all in. There's no going back."

"I'm going through a divorce and my dick of an ex-husband wants alimony plus half of my business. Can you believe that? I built this company from the ground up while he went to college then law school. He hasn't given me a dime since he left, but he has money to take his assistant to Paris. The kids need braces, and I'm about to lose my house. It's a chance I'm willing to take." She rolls her lips together. "Of course, I expect to be compensated accordingly."

We work out a deal and make plans for our first job. The next day, Em purchases burner phones for the three of us. I make the five-hour drive to St. Louis in search of someone to turn our goods into cash. By the end of the week, I have photos for my next set of forgeries, a buyer for our merchandise, and a solid plan to evict Cash from my life.

In the meantime, sales at Mercer's continue to lag. At this rate, we won't be able to cover payroll next month. Mr. Mercer's health continues to decline, and I can't bring myself to bother him with our problems. With a heavy heart, I make the difficult decision to cut back the store hours and liquidate some of the inventory. When the artists arrive to reclaim their consignment works, my simmering anger toward Cash ignites into a furious inferno. I was counting on at least a few sales from the trade show to bolster our finances through this rough patch. His meddling has put my future—and the futures of those who depend on me—in jeopardy.

My world becomes a whirlwind of running the store, making forgeries, and plotting revenge against the tattooed devil. At night, I relive our tryst on the balcony while touching myself. My hatred mingles with desire in a combination more potent than anything I've ever experienced. I don't know if I want to fuck him or kill him—maybe both. Not at the same time, because that would be creepy.

At the end of the month, Loretta texts me on the burner phone. A downtown Indianapolis coffee shop is the location for our first drop. We carry identical tote bags. Mine carries cash for her payment. Hers holds the jewels. We make the swap beneath the table. To anyone watching, we're just two friends catching up over espresso and muffins. After a chat about her kids and the latest celebrity gossip, she leaves. I drive to St. Louis and convert the stolen pieces to money. Although the conversion rate is less than I'd like, it's a start.

After two more jobs, I've got his payment in full. I send him a text. No answer. I keep texting because I'm eager for this charade to be over, yet he continues to ignore me. Another week passes, then two. I walk through the days on pins and needles, certain he's going to show up when I least expect it.

On Saturday evening, Emeline has a date with Tony so it's my turn to close up at the store. My nightly routine begins as usual. I go to the front, lock the door, turn the sign, and head back to my office. When I flip on the overhead light, he's there, sitting behind my desk, sexy and smoldering in his jeans and hoodie. I gasp in surprise. The sight of him elicits conflicting emotions. My heart jumps into my throat while my panties dampen. I hate myself for letting him scare me. I hate myself more for wanting him anyway.

"Where have you been?" I ask, not bothering to hide my irritation. "Please take your feet off my desk. Don't you have any manners?"

"The heat's been on. Had to lay low for a while." He removes his feet, letting them thump on the floor in exaggerated compliance, then leans forward, resting his elbows on his thighs. "I figured you'd be grateful for the extra time."

"What do you mean by heat?" My heart continues to run a ragged race. I lean back against the wall and cross my arms over my chest to hide the telltale jut of my nipples against my blouse.

"The feds, darlin'. They've been all over me for the past few weeks. You don't happen to know anything about that, do you?" He stands, a picture of easy grace and confidence, and stalks toward me.

"No. Why would I?" With every stride closer to me, my resolve to end our physical relationship weakens. His lips are redder than usual, outlined by the thin strip of his moustache. I can't help remembering how good his mouth felt on mine, the taste of peppermint on his tongue, the way he owned my body after a single kiss.

His wide shoulders lift and drop in a casual shrug. "No idea. Never hurts to ask."

"Maybe you've been a little sloppy in your business. Can't be too careful these days." I can't help but taunt him. Yanking his chain is the only form of retaliation available to me.

"Yeah?" His stare locks onto my mouth. "And what would you know about that?" By now, his face is inches from my nose. I stare up at him, mesmerized by the strong lines of his features, the straight nose, and his square jaw with just the right amount of scruff on it. He braces a hand on the wall beside my head.

I melt beneath the heat in his gaze. "Not a thing."

"So, you got my money, little girl?" He brushes the hair from my face, leaning in closer.

I uncross my arms, let my hands fall to my sides, press my palms to the wall at my back, and wait. His nearness electrifies every nerve ending in my body. I'm acutely aware of the rise and fall of his chest and the intoxicating scent of his cologne. I swallow through the tightness in my throat before speaking. "Yes. It's in the vault. Let me get it."

When he doesn't move, I duck beneath his arm. Even though my back is to him, I can feel the burn of his gaze on my backside. I like having him watch me, knowing his full attention is mine and mine alone. My fingers shake as I twist the dial of the combination lock on the vault. I withdraw a duffel bag, close the door, and toss it on the floor in front of him. "It's all there."

"All of it?" His eyebrows rise. The denim of his jeans stretches tight as he squats in front of the bag. He draws down the zipper to peek inside and ruffles through the stacks of bills.

"Yes. Plus interest." I exhale a breath of relief, exhilarated to have this nightmare come to a close. "You can count it."

"No need. I trust you." He closes the duffel and stands, draws the strap over his shoulder. "Where did you get the money?"

"Not your business," I reply, throwing his own words back at him.

"Fair enough." He stares at me. For the first time, I see a flicker of emotion in his eyes. If I didn't know better, I'd swear it was regret. Instead of leaving, he walks up to me, stopping when he's close enough to reveal the gold flecks in his brown irises. "Well, I guess this is it then."

"Yes."

"Unless you want to take this back to your bedroom for a celebration."

The rusty growl in his offer hits me right between the legs. I'm instantly wet and ready. My mouth is so dry, I can barely swallow. I clear my throat. "No. We're done."

"Shame." He studies my face like he's memorizing every feature. "I was getting used to having you around." Using his pinky, he sweeps the hair away from my forehead, trails his fingers along my jaw, my neck, my collarbone. A heavy sigh gusts from my lips. "All right then. See ya around, Jagger Jones."

FOURTEEN

Jagger

Paying my debt to Cash should've been the end of my relationship with Loretta, but we decide to keep going. We agree to meet for the final exchange on the first Thursday in June at an outdoor café in Carmel.

To make sure I'm not followed, I hide my car in a parking garage and walk the two blocks to the restaurant. We have salads and talk about the new shopping mall going up down the street, the traffic congestion on the interstate.

"There's no point in getting greedy," Loretta says when we're finished eating. She hauls the strap of her cash-filled tote over her shoulder. Her smile is blinding. "We had a good run, Jagger Jones. It's been good doing business with you."

"You, too." We share a hug before heading in separate directions.

I walk to my car with the tote bag of jewels tucked

beneath my arm. Overhead, white fluffy clouds float in a soft blue sky. Baskets of sweet-smelling flowers hang from the black cast iron streetlamps. The houses lining the street have pristine lawns, manicured hedges, and expensive cars in their driveways.

The only thing more perfect than my surroundings is the heady intoxication of success. We did it. I beat Cash, repaid Callie's debt, and have enough merchandise in my bag to get Mercer's back on its feet.

Inside the parking garage, I pause on the third level in front of the spot where I *thought* my Honda should be sitting. An elegant Mercedes sedan is there instead. I chuckle to myself at the memory lapse and search for a familiar landmark. The fire extinguisher. The elevator. Everything seems right, yet my car isn't anywhere to be seen. A sense of unease prickles along the back of my neck.

"Lose something?" The voice behind me is familiar, unsettling, and deep.

This *canno*t be happening. I turn in a slow circle.

"So how do you like my new car?" Cash sits in the driver's seat of a red, vintage convertible roadster with shiny chrome and sparkling wire wheels. The wrist of his right arm rests on the top of the steering wheel. His opposite elbow lounges on the windowsill. His neck tattoo is on full display above the collar of his black T-shirt. He jerks his head toward the passenger side. "Hop in. Let's go for a drive."

A quick glance to my left and right confirms that

we're alone on this level. "I'm not going anywhere with you ever again."

His familiar chuckle is both frightening and thrilling. A boyish grin reveals his dimples. "Never say never, sweet thing." When I don't budge, he arches an eyebrow. "Wanna show me what you got in that bag?"

I clutch the bag tighter against my midriff. He couldn't possibly know, could he? "Why are you here?"

"Always so many questions." He shakes his head. "'Why are you here? Where are we going? What are you doing?'" The smile slips from his face. "I know what you've been up to, Jagger Jones." He leans across the car, opens the passenger door, and pats the leather seat. "Get in the car, hot stuff. I don't want to shout our business for everyone to hear."

Once again, I'm at a crossroads. The smart thing to do would be run or scream. I do neither. Instead, I slide into the bucket seat. Deep down, I'm thrilled to see him again. I have no idea where he's taking me, but it's guaranteed to be one hell of a ride. Seeing him now, here, rekindles my attraction. If I'm honest with myself, I've never stopped thinking about him.

"Fine. But I only have an hour." My attention is drawn to his tattooed fingers as he works the manual gearshift. There's something strong and sexy about a man behind the wheel of a growling sportscar. His large body overpowers the cockpit of the small roadster. We drive through the quiet streets. The wind whips my hair. I gather it into a ponytail and draw it to one side.

"Have you ever heard an engine purr like that before?" he asks as he merges onto the interstate. With a pump of the clutch and a shift of gears, the car rockets forward. We weave in and out of traffic along I-465. When the skyscrapers of downtown come into view, he takes the Ohio Street exit and heads toward Monument Circle.

"This is insane," I mutter.

"I know, right?" He shakes his head, a smirk on his face. "This is a 1974 Jaguar E-Type. All original. Only twenty-seven thousand miles on the odometer. They don't make them like this anymore."

"I meant your behavior."

"Oh, yeah." His dimples are on full display. I can't help glancing at his handsome profile. I've never seen him so relaxed or so gleeful. He catches my gaze. "You gotta forgive me. Cars are my passion. I get excited, you know?"

"You didn't hijack my afternoon to drive me around Indianapolis. What is it you want?" My patience is growing thin. The longer I'm around him, the more I like him. I don't want to like him. I want to hate him.

"When I saw this car, I thought damn, Jagger would look great in that. Red's a good color for you." At the stoplight, he rests an elbow on the center console and leans toward me.

For a fraction of a second, I have a premonition of what life as his girlfriend might be like. Then I shove it away, because I know it's never going to happen. I won't let it. "I don't have time for this, Cash. Get to the point."

He huffs an exasperated sigh. "Fine." The light changes, and we're on the move again. "Here's the deal. I know what you got going on with your homegirl Loretta, and I want in on it."

My heart sinks. The bliss of the day floats away on the warm breeze. "How? How could you possibly know?"

"I got friends all over, Jagger." At the next intersection, the stoplight turns red. We stop again. He drops a hand on my knee and squeezes, sending ripples of delight up my leg. "So here's how this is going to go down. You're going to stop taking your merchandise to that slimy St. Louis sleaze ball and bring it straight to me."

I stare out the windshield at the crazy throng of traffic, the pedestrians, and the Soldiers and Sailors monument ahead of us. How did I get here again? I clear my throat. "We're done. *I'm* done."

"No, no, darlin'." His laughter both warms and terrifies me. "You ain't done 'til I say you're done, and we're just getting started." He brushes the hair away from my face with a gentle sweep. Those warm brown eyes lock on my lips. "You and me—we're partners now. Fifty-fifty split. I'm gonna make you rich, angel."

"I want to be done," I whisper. "This kind of life isn't for me. I don't want this." The words are a lie. Need swells inside me, threatening to crack my ribs. I want what he has. I want his wealth, this car, his power. Temptation curls around my soul and tugs. With Cash at my side, the possibilities for my future are limitless.

"Sure you do." He sees through my dishonesty. As always, he knows what I want before I do.

"What if I don't? What if I want to be a normal girl with a normal job?" Excitement hums through my blood.

He's quiet as he makes a left turn then casts a sideways glance at me. "We both know you're better than that."

"Why do you keep doing this?" Another red light brings our progress to a halt. I run a hand over the seat, feeling the heat of the sun in the leather, wondering what it would be like to own something this beautiful.

"I'm a bad guy, darlin', and bad guys do bad things." At the intersection of Meridian and Ohio, he sets the parking brake and hops over the car door, landing lightly on the street.

"Cash!" I stare at him, mouth agape.

Over his shoulder, he says, "Keep the car. You look good in it." His shit-eating grin is back. He winks. "Consider it a token of my good faith in our new business venture, partner. I'll be in touch." With those final words, he weaves between the cars and melts into the people on the sidewalk on the opposite side of the street, leaving me alone and driverless.

I'm too stunned for the first few seconds to comprehend what just happened. The traffic light switches from red to green. Behind me the long line of traffic grows impatient. Horns honk. Someone yells. I quickly unfasten my seatbelt and slide behind the steering wheel. I circle the block, thinking he has to be near, but he's nowhere to be found.

In the space of thirty minutes, he's managed to worm his way back into my life. My hands tremble as I clutch the steering wheel. We're going to be partners. He values me. Me. Little Jagger Jones from nowhere. I blow out a breath to sweep away the anxiety. I have no idea what to do next, so I drive toward home.

The car is stunning. It's been years since I've driven a manual transmission. For the first few blocks, the car hops when I shift gears. After a few minutes, I get the hang of the clutch. On the interstate, I shove the accelerator to the floor and revel in the power of the engine. Under different circumstances I would be thrilled to receive a gift like this, but I know there are strings attached. Long, indestructible, life-altering strings. Once Cash is back in my life, I'll never be able to get rid of him. I tried so hard to escape his grasp, but I enjoyed every minute of the struggle.

When I pull into the driveway at home, there's an unfamiliar car parked on the street in front of the house. I don't pay too much attention. Maybe someone is visiting Mrs. Johnson across the street. I'm more concerned with how I'm gonna explain the classic convertible to Emeline. She won't be happy to know Cash is back in our lives. I sit in the car for a few minutes before going inside to prepare my story. I promised never to lie to her again, and I won't.

After a deep, cleansing breath, I head inside and drop the car keys in the bowl by the door. When I turn around, I see Em is sitting on the couch in the living room, her back stiff, complexion pale.

"Hey," I say.

"Hello," she replies. The strangeness in her tone grabs my attention.

"You won't believe what happened to–" I don't get a chance to finish the sentence. A man steps into my line of sight, previously hidden by the wall between the foyer and living room. His brown hair and pleasant features are familiar.

"Ms. Jones, hello. It's nice to see you again." He extends his hand to shake. I stare at it. After a beat, he drops it to his side, flexing his fingers. "You're surprised. We met in Vegas. Remember?"

"Wayne?" He's the guy from the hotel club. No wonder Em is freaked out. What kind of creepy stalker tracks a woman across an entire country after a ten-minute conversation? I back toward the door, mind racing, trying to remember if my phone is in my purse or still in the car. "This is unexpected."

"It's Warren, actually. Special Agent Will Warren." He takes a step toward me and flips open his wallet to reveal a shield and picture ID. Federal Bureau of Investigations. FBI. A second man comes out of the hall bathroom. Both are wearing dark trousers, a button-down shirt and tie, sensible black shoes. Warren gestures toward his companion. "This is my partner, Agent Dodd."

"I—I don't understand." I glance at Em. She's still as a statue, hands clasped in her lap, knuckles white.

Warren has the good grace to look embarrassed. "I know this must be a shock to you. Why don't you sit down?"

"No. I'm fine." An unpleasant burning sensation races through my veins. "What's this about?"

Agent Dodd walks to the window, sweeps the curtains aside with two fingers, and lets out a low whistle. "That's some car you've got there, Ms. Jones. What is that? An Aston Martin? Seventies?"

"It's a 1974 Jaguar E-Type," I reply.

"A car like that has to cost a pretty penny. I'm surprised you can afford such an expensive car, considering the financial problems your business has been facing." Agent Dodd is older than Warren, maybe mid-forties. Threads of gray highlight his sideburns. His forehead furrows in confusion as he turns to his partner. "Doesn't Cash Delacorte have a car like that?"

"You know, I think he does," Warren replies. "You don't happen to know him, do you, Ms. Jones?"

I choose not to answer. A wave of calm sweeps over me. I snap out of my funk and move toward the kitchen. "I'm so sorry. Where are my manners? Would anyone like some coffee or a glass of water?"

Warren steps into my path. "We're fine. Please sit down, Ms. Jones." His next words turn my world upside down. "We'd like to ask you some questions about your part in the extortion and murder of Hubert Spillman."

ABSOLUTE
TRUST

USA TODAY BESTSELLING AUTHOR
JEANA E. MANN

READY FOR ABSOLUTE TRUST?

I'm just a simple girl from a poor background, who loves with all her heart and has the best of intentions. Falling in love with Cash Delacorte was never a life goal. The former gang leader turned ruthless billionaire holds all of my power. He owns me—body, soul, and bank account.

The problem? I like it. I crave his touch in the dark of night. I long to hear his whispered dirty words in my ear when we make love. Most of all, I trust him to do what's right for me. Because that's what we do when we're in love, right? We trust the wrong people. We make bad decisions. And we sacrifice our souls to make them happy.

Now, with the FBI breathing down our necks and a million dollars in stolen jewels on the line, the power rests in my hands. One word from me can bring Cash's empire crashing down around him. Does he trust me enough to save us both or will his need for power ruin the only love I've ever known?

USA Today bestselling author Jeana E. Mann brings the heat in this dark and suspenseful romance.

This is BOOK TWO of a duet and is intended to be read after ABSOLUTE POWER.

These books are written in the worlds of THE EXILED PRINCE TRILOGY, THE REBEL QUEEN DUET, and THE RUTHLESS KNIGHT. You do not need to read the other books to enjoy the ABSOLUTE POWER DUET.

99 CENT PREORDER SPECIAL

Absolute Trust

Release day 7/7/20

Also by Jeana E. Mann

The Rich Royal and Ruthless Collection

(In reading order)

THE EXILED PRINCE TRILOGY

The Exiled Prince

The Dirty Princess

The War King

THE REBEL QUEEN DUET

The Royal Arrangement

The Rebel Queen

STANDALONE

The Ruthless Knight

THE ABSOLUTE POWER DUET

Absolute Power

Absolute Trust

PRETTY BROKEN SERIES

(In reading order)

Pretty Broken Girl

Pretty Filthy Lies

Pretty Dirty Secrets

Pretty Wild Thing

Pretty Broken Promises

Pretty Broken Dreams

Pretty Broken Baby

Pretty Broken Hearts

Pretty Broken Bastard

―――――

FELONY ROMANCE SERIES

Intoxicated

Unexpected

Vindicated

Impulsive

Drift

Committed

―――――

STANDALONES

Lies We Tell

Dirty Work

―――――

SHORT STORIES

<u>Everything</u>

<u>Linger</u>

About the Author

Jeana is a *USA Today* and *Publishers Weekly* bestselling author from Indiana. She gave up a career in the corporate world to write about sexy billionaires and alpha bad boys. With over twenty books, three series, and many awards beneath her belt, she's never regretted her choice to live out her dream. She's a free spirit, a wanderer at heart, and loves animals with a passion. When she's not tripping over random objects, you'll find her walking in the sunshine with her rambunctious dogs and dreaming about true love. Subscribe to Jeana's newsletter and get the inside scoop on new and upcoming releases, giveaways, and much more! SUBSCRIBE

TEXT ALERTS -
text the word "Jeana" without quotation marks to 21000 and get new release alerts straight to your phone.

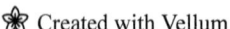

9 781943 938544